PORPOISE IN THE POOL

As before, the porpoise stopped just short of the edge. Briefly, she lifted her head and looked out to sea, then she turned and swam to the far end of the pool.

'It's as if she's afraid to make the leap to freedom,' said Janet Gill, shaking her head in disbelief.

Another enormous wave was rolling towards the rockpool.

'Look, Morveren!' cried Mandy. 'This one will help to lift you out. You *must* go now!' Her voice rang out above the thundering water. The little porpoise lifted her head and looked up at the rock where everyone stood. With an intense stare, she looked straight into Mandy's eyes.

Mandy's heart skipped a beat. 'Go, Morveren!' she cried again. 'GO!'

LUCY DANIELS

Porpoise
— in the —
Pool

Illustrations by Ann Baum

*Hodder
Children's
Books*

a division of Hodder Headline Limited

Special thanks to Linda Chapman

**Thanks also to Vanessa Williams for reviewing
the information in this book**

Animal Ark is a trademark of Working Partners Limited
Text copyright © 2001 Working Partners Limited
Created by Working Partners Limited, London W6 0QT
Original series created by Ben M. Baglio
Illustrations copyright © 2001 Ann Baum

First published in Great Britain in 2001
by Hodder Children's Books

For more information about Animal Ark,
please contact www.animalark.co.uk

10 9 8 7 6 5 4 3 2 1

A Catalogue record for this book is available from the British Library

ISBN 0 340 79555 7

Typeset by Avon Dataset Ltd, Bidford-on-Avon, Warks

Printed and bound in Great Britain by
Clays Ltd, St Ives plc

Hodder Children's Books
a division of Hodder Headline Limited
338 Euston Road
London NW1 3BH

One

'I always think it's just like squeezing into a new skin!' Mandy Hope laughed as she pushed an arm into the sleeve of her wetsuit.

'Yes – one that's a size too small,' grunted James Hunter, struggling to pull his wetsuit above his waist. The two friends were on the beach, preparing themselves for a day of surfing. James had never worn a wetsuit before so he hadn't yet mastered how to put it on. He twisted and wriggled, then let out a groan. 'Oh no! There's sand in it. I'll have to start all over again!'

Mandy grinned as James peeled off the tight

rubber gear. 'It looks like you're shedding your skin, like a snake!'

James pulled a face, then stepped out of his wetsuit and shook it out. Trying not to kick sand back into it, he stepped into the suit again. 'I wish our own skins were thick enough to keep us warm in the sea,' he grumbled.

'You'd have to have a layer of blubber under it, like a whale, to stop you from freezing when you're surfing in the Atlantic Ocean!' chuckled Joshua Gill, who was kneeling on the beach rubbing wax on to a surfboard.

Mandy and James were spending part of their summer holiday with eleven-year-old Joshua. He and his parents, Chris and Janet Gill, and older brother, Ed, lived in Sennen Cove near Land's End in Cornwall. Chris Gill was a vet, like Mandy's father, Adam Hope. The two men had been friends since training together at veterinary college.

Mandy's mother, Emily Hope, was also a vet. The Hopes ran a veterinary practice, Animal Ark, attached to their home in the Yorkshire village of Welford.

'Sorry the suit's a bit small,' said Josh, as James

battled to get his arms into the sleeves. Unlike Mandy, James did not have his own wetsuit, so Josh had lent him one. 'I'll see if I can find a bigger one next time we come surfing,' Josh added.

Josh was a very keen surfer. He spent most of his spare time at Whitesands Beach – a long sandy beach popular with surfers. He had promised to help Mandy and James learn how to surf too.

Josh stood up and looked at the waves. 'It's looking great!' he said enthusiastically. 'We'll have some really cool rides today.'

'Not like that one, I hope,' Mandy joked, as she saw a surfer tumble off his board and a large wave crash down on to him.

'We'll probably all get dumped like that once or twice.' Josh grinned.

'Even when we're starting with boogie-boards?' James asked warily. He had never been surfing before and wanted to take it slowly.

'Even when we're starting with boogie-boards,' echoed Josh. 'They might be smaller than surfboards but you can still get dumped,' he said, grinning. 'So be prepared for some rough rides.'

Mandy put up a hand to shield her eyes from the glare of the sun on the water and looked out to sea. A large group of surfers was waiting patiently beyond the breakers for a good wave. When a large swell started to build up behind the surfers, two of them turned their boards to face the shore and started to paddle rapidly. The swell quickly caught up with them and began to break. As the top of the wave curled over, the pair stood up on their boards and were soon being pushed along by the powerful surge of water.

'They're really good,' said James, admiringly, as the surfers shot towards the shore. He turned to Josh. 'I expect you're an expert too.'

'Not really,' Josh told him. He picked up his surfboard. 'I'm OK on a boogie-board but I haven't had my surfboard very long. It used to be Ed's. He gave it to me at the start of the summer and I've only just learned to stand on it. Up until then I always surfed with a boogie-board.'

Mandy and James hadn't met sixteen-year-old Ed yet. He had gone out before they arrived that morning.

'Doesn't he surf any more?' asked Mandy. She had heard that Ed, like his mother, was very keen on photography. Perhaps he had given up surfing so that he could spend more time taking photographs.

'No,' said Josh. 'He's into jetskiing now.' He wrinkled his nose. 'He says surfing is much too tame for him.'

'Jetskiing!' echoed James. 'That's awesome. Does he have his own jetski?'

Josh nodded. 'Uh-huh. It's just about the most important thing in his life at the moment. He wanted it so badly that he worked on a friend's fishing boat every Saturday for two years as well as every day in the holidays to earn the money to buy it.' As he spoke, he frowned.

'Are you saving up for one, too?' asked James.

'Not on your life!' said Josh, emphatically.

Mandy was puzzled by the abruptness of his answer but before she could ask him what he meant, Josh changed the subject. 'Come on,' he said. 'We're missing some great waves. Let's get out there.' With his surfboard under one arm, he headed for the water.

James took off his glasses and left them in his sports bag on the beach, along with the rest of their kit. Then Mandy and James each picked up a boogie-board and ran to join Josh in the sea.

'Do you want to practise in the shallow water for a while until you get the hang of it?' asked Josh.

'Good idea,' said Mandy. She had done some boogie-boarding when she had been in Australia for six months, but she felt she needed some time to get back into the swing of it. She glanced at the large waves the surfers were riding further out to sea. It was going to be great to experience the thrill of the surf again.

Suddenly she saw something else on the far side of the bay, riding the waves. 'Oh, look! Dolphins!' she gasped, identifying the sleek, dark shapes speeding down a huge swell.

Like torpedoes, the dolphins hurtled down the wall of water. Then, just as the swell was starting to curl over at the top and break, they leaped high into the air and plunged back into the sea behind the wave.

'And they're so close to the surfers! Isn't that brilliant!' cried Mandy, ecstatically. 'I wish I was out there with them.'

Josh laughed. 'The surf must be really good if the dolphins are riding it too.'

'What kind of dolphins are they?' asked James.

'Probably bottlenoses,' Josh told him. 'We see them quite often in Sennen Cove. They love body-surfing, as you can see, but they also like riding in the wash made by the fishing boats. When they surf at the front of a boat it's called bow-riding, and at the back it's called wake-riding.'

Mandy was delighted. She had hoped they would see some marine wildlife during their stay in Cornwall and already – less than a day into their holiday – they had been treated to a dolphin 'show'.

'Do you think we'll see any other marine mammals, Josh?' asked Mandy, as she watched the dolphins heading back out to sea. It seemed they had grown tired of body-surfing and were off to find something else to do. Mandy wouldn't be surfing alongside them today.

Josh shrugged his shoulders. 'Probably,' he said. 'We might see basking sharks and minke whales off-shore. And if we're very lucky we may get a sighting of harbour porpoises.'

'Why do you say lucky?' asked Mandy. She remembered the porpoises she and James had spotted from a boat on Loch Ferran in Scotland.

The porpoises had followed a shoal of mackerel into the loch and had been very easy to see as they rolled and dived through the water after the fish.

'Well, harbour porpoises are quite small and they're really shy,' explained Josh. 'They don't show much of themselves at the surface. And they don't body-surf or bow-ride like the dolphins. But who knows? We might just get a glimpse of one today.' He hauled himself on to his surfboard. 'Come on,' he said eagerly. 'Surf's up!'

Mandy lay on her stomach on the boogie-board and paddled out a short way next to Josh. James stayed close to shore and practised catching small waves in the shallows.

'Take this one,' called Josh to Mandy when the next wave rolled towards them.

Mandy turned her board and started paddling towards the beach. Suddenly she felt herself being propelled forward by the surging water. 'This is great!' she yelled as she shot past James and skidded to a halt on the wet sand. She leaped to her feet and dashed back into the sea. 'Come on, James!' she shouted encouragingly. He was still testing himself in water that was only knee-deep. 'Come further out. The waves are stronger and it's really easy,' she said.

'OK,' called James. 'Wait for me.' He flopped on to the board and paddled out after Mandy. Ahead of them, a big wave broke and came crashing towards them. Mandy remembered just what to do. She pushed down hard on the board, took a deep breath, and dived under the foaming water. She felt the wave tumbling above her then she came back up to the surface and saw the breaker burst on to the shore, surging against the people playing in the shallows.

But the wave wasn't all that washed up on to the sand. A blue boogie-board bounced along in the swirling water, then came to a standstill on the beach. It looked like James's board. But where was James? Anxiously, Mandy glanced around for him, then spotted a figure being washed on to the shore not far from the boogie-board.

'Poor James,' said Mandy to herself as she watched him sit up and wipe his hair out of his eyes. A small wave built up behind her. She caught it and steered her board towards her friend.

'Sorry,' she said as she came to a stop in front of him. 'I should have told you what to do about breakers like that.' She stifled a laugh as James

blinked at her, then wiped sand from his eyes and mouth.

'What *do* you do?' spluttered James with a weak grin.

'You've got to push yourself under the wave,' came Josh's voice.

Mandy hadn't noticed him surfing in behind her.

'Sorry, James,' he apologised. 'I forgot you haven't boogie-boarded before. I'll help you to get the hang of it.'

'Thanks,' said James, gratefully. He stood up and grinned broadly. 'Trust me to be the first one to get dumped! Just as well I didn't have my glasses on,' he said with a chuckle.

Mandy smiled at James. He was such a good sport.

Josh pushed his surfboard towards Mandy. 'Let's swap,' he said. 'It's best if James and I are both on boogie-boards.'

Hesitantly, Mandy reached for the bigger board. She really wanted to have a go at proper surfing but wasn't sure she was ready for it yet.

Josh seemed to notice her reluctance. 'You'll be OK,' he said reassuringly. 'You were pretty good on the boogie-board so you should get the hang of surfing quite quickly. You just have to work at getting your balance.'

Mandy grimaced. 'Just how do you stand up on something the size of a plank, when you're riding big waves like those?' she asked.

Josh laughed. 'Well, you don't do that straight away. Start by lying on the board on your tummy. Then, when you've got the feel of it, you can try kneeling when a wave comes. That's how I learned to do it.'

Mandy looked at him doubtfully. 'You make it sound very easy,' she said, pulling herself on to the board. She grabbed the leash that was attached to the keel of the board and looped it round her ankle. 'Oh well, I guess I'll be the next one to be dumped,' she said. She lay down and began paddling slowly away from the shore. At least the leash would ensure that she didn't lose the board if she was washed off it.

'It's not that bad being dumped,' said James behind her. 'All you have to do is make sure that your eyes and mouth are closed!'

Mandy looked at him over her shoulder and grinned. 'Thanks for the good advice!'

'Here comes a small wave,' shouted Josh. 'Turn round and give it a try.'

Mandy manoeuvred the board round to face the shore. The wave rippled towards her. She paddled hard then suddenly felt the board being lifted by the wave. *Got it!* she thought excitedly. She stopped paddling and, still lying on her stomach, held the sides of the board and steered it through the other surfers until she came to a stop on the sand.

Mandy was exhilarated. 'I did it!' she yelled

triumphantly. She had caught her first wave on a real surfboard.

James and Josh applauded her loudly. 'Now you've just got to learn to stand. Then you'll be hooked for life,' Josh warned her.

'Unless you move on to jetskiing,' remarked James.

'Jetskiing's not a patch on surfing,' said Josh seriously. Then more light-heartedly, he said, 'OK, James. Let's turn you into an ace boogie-boarder.'

While Josh showed James when to start paddling and how to deal with tricky waves, Mandy practised in the shallows on the bigger board. She tried to keep away from all the other surfers so that she wouldn't bump into them.

It wasn't long before Mandy felt confident enough to kneel on the board. *I have to give it a try sometime*, she said to herself as she folded her legs beneath her and started paddling just ahead of a small wave. But as she felt the swell gathering her up, she began to wobble. Within seconds, she had lost her balance completely. 'Oops!' she moaned as she plunged into the churning water. The next thing she knew, she was sitting on the beach, her hair and mouth full of sand!

James and Joshua had watched her progress. 'Are you all right, Mandy?' called Josh.

'Fine!' called back Mandy, rising to her feet and spitting the sand out of her mouth.

James pointed to his mouth. 'I told you to keep it closed,' he said, grinning.

Mandy laughed and picked up the surfboard. She headed back into the sea, determined to do better next time.

After a few more wobbly attempts, Mandy found her balance. Soon she had learned how to kneel up on the board, and how to steer the board with the weight of her body. Josh was right. She was hooked!

Mandy glanced at James. She saw that he had overcome his earlier clumsiness on the boogie-board and was easily catching waves. *He'll be hooked too, before long*, she thought, smiling to herself.

Encouraged by her own progress, Mandy decided to venture further out to tackle some bigger waves. It was rather tricky paddling out through the breakers but eventually she found herself in deeper, calmer water.

This is far enough, she told herself. *I'll wait here for a good-sized swell*. The experienced surfers were even further out to sea but Mandy knew she wasn't ready to join them yet. She lay on her board, enjoying the peaceful rocking motion of the water.

Resting her chin in her hands, Mandy gazed out to sea. The vast Atlantic Ocean stretched away to the horizon, glinting in the summer sun. Animal Ark seemed so far away. She tried to imagine what was happening at the surgery at that moment, and pictured a room full of animals and their owners waiting to see her parents.

As these thoughts drifted through her mind, Mandy became aware of a sharp, puffing sound. It sounded a bit like a fast sneeze. She listened carefully. The noise was repeated. What could it be?

Mandy sat up on the board and looked around. The sea was flat and calm.

Choo came the noise again and it was followed by a long, drawn-out *pherrh*, which sounded almost like a heavy sigh.

Squinting, Mandy looked out across the shimmering water in the direction of the noise. As her eyes became accustomed to the glare, she thought she could make out a number of dark shapes floating just below the surface, about fifty metres to her left.

Mandy kept very still. If she wasn't mistaken, she was looking at a group of basking marine mammals!

There was another sharp puff, then one of the shapes rose quietly to the surface. For a split second it broke the surface of the water before disappearing again. Mandy's heart leaped. In that brief moment, she had spotted a small blunt-tipped fin. *Harbour porpoises!* she thought in amazement. *I think I'm looking at a pod of harbour porpoises!*

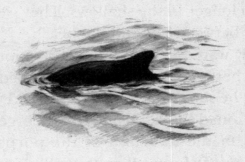

Two

A shiver of excitement ran through Mandy. Josh had said how shy the porpoises were, yet here she was not very far away from a group of them! She craned her neck to try to see them more clearly. Even though they were lying below the surface of the water, Mandy could see that they were quite small – less than two metres long – but broad and strong looking.

Moving very slowly so as not to disturb the porpoises, she turned the surfboard round. The sea was packed with surfers but she could make out the tall, thin figure of Joshua. He and James were no longer in the shallows. They were about halfway between her and the beach.

Mandy waved to attract their attention. Joshua noticed her and waved back. Mandy beckoned to him but he shook his head and pointed to James. She beckoned again, this time more urgently, and pointed in the direction of the porpoises. *He probably thinks I want them to come out here just to catch waves,* she thought. What a surprise they were in for!

James and Joshua exchanged a few words then began to paddle out to her. As they approached, Mandy put a finger to her lips to warn them to be quiet. At once they began to paddle more slowly, barely making a splash.

James looked puzzled. He frowned at Mandy and mouthed, 'What is it?'

Mandy pointed to the porpoises again. 'Porpoises,' she mouthed back.

'What did you say?' whispered James, coming alongside her.

'Porpoises, I think,' Mandy murmured. 'Over there, just below the surface. You can see some dark shapes.'

James squinted. 'I wish I had my glasses on,' he

muttered. 'I can't see very much. Just some black blobs.'

'That's about all I can see, too,' said Mandy quietly.

Pherrh. Another puffing sigh broke the silence.

Joshua, floating on his board on the other side of Mandy, whistled softly. 'You're right!' he breathed in astonishment. 'They *are* porpoises. Harbour porpoises. That sound is the blow. When other marine mammals like whales breathe out you see the spout of water coming out of their blowhole, but you won't see it with porpoises.'

Choo! came another fast blow. Josh shook his head as if he couldn't believe what he was seeing and hearing.

'They look a bit like logs floating in the water,' whispered James, peering at them through half-closed eyes.

'I guess that's why it's called "logging" when marine mammals float like that,' said Josh, grinning. 'And do you know? This is the first time I've seen it for real.'

Mandy smiled at him. 'You *said* we'd be very lucky to spot harbour porpoises,' she reminded him.

'We are,' Josh said quietly. 'And I can't believe that you've only been in Sennen Cove for half a day and already you've seen a whole pod!'

James glanced at Mandy and, with a muffled laugh, said, 'It's always like that when Mandy's around. She attracts animals!'

Mandy liked the idea of being a magnet for animals. She hoped that would always be the case because when she grew up she was going to be a vet, just like her parents.

There was a slight ripple in the water, followed by a flash of white at the surface.

'What was that?' breathed James.

'I think one of the porpoises was turning over,' Josh explained. 'The white flash must have been its belly. Sometimes porpoises roll over while they're basking.'

There came a few more rolls then the pod settled down again. Mandy tried to count the shapes. 'I think there are about six of them,' she whispered to Josh and James.

'That's about the normal size for a group,' said Josh.

The porpoises looked very peaceful as they rested silently just beneath the surface. If it hadn't

been for the noise of the blow, Mandy would probably never have known they were there.

'How do you know they're harbour porpoises and not dolphins, Josh?' asked James.

'Well, first of all, porpoises are much smaller than the dolphins in this area,' said Josh. 'Also, if you spot a dorsal fin, you'll see that it's not hooked like a dolphin's,' he explained in a low voice.

'I saw a fin when I first spotted the group,' whispered Mandy. 'It was small and blunt.'

Josh nodded. 'That's how one of my books describes them,' he said. 'Their heads are different too,' he went on. 'Dolphins have a beak but harbour porpoises have rounded heads.'

'I wish one would lift its head out of the water,' said Mandy softly.

'Or even its whole body!' remarked James.

Josh shook his head. 'I don't think that will happen,' he said. 'You see, they're also different in that way. Dolphins leap right out of the water – like we saw them doing earlier when they were body-surfing. But porpoises aren't usually very acrobatic. When they move, they look as if they're rolling along on wheels.'

'Oh yes! I've seen that sort of movement. That's

how the porpoises swam in Loch Ferran,' recalled James. 'You really know a lot about marine animals, Josh,' he added.

'Well, next to surfing, that's my main hobby,' Josh told him. 'My dad's keen on marine wildlife too. I've learned a lot from him.'

'Shhh,' whispered Mandy. The porpoises were stirring slightly. She was afraid that all the talking might be upsetting them. But as she watched, she saw that the disturbance was not because they were afraid. It was caused by two tiny calves. The little grey creatures were barely half a metre long, but Mandy caught a fleeting glimpse of them at the surface before they vanished among the pod once more. 'Wow!' she gasped. 'Calves! Did you see them?'

'I think so,' said James, squinting towards the porpoises.

'That was amazing!' said Josh with a broad smile.

'Do you think we've come across a porpoise nursery?' asked Mandy.

'Could be,' said Josh. 'It *is* the breeding season after all. Dad told me that porpoises rear their calves quite close to shore.' He pointed to a headland jutting out to sea not far to their left. 'You'll probably find those cliffs give them some shelter so they feel quite safe here,' he said. He looked wistfully back at the little group of animals. 'I wish the calves would surface again,' he said.

'I'm surprised our boards haven't scared them off,' said James.

Mandy nodded. She was starting to feel anxious that they might be intruding on the porpoises' territory. 'I hope they don't see us as a threat,' she said. 'Especially as there are calves in the pod.'

Josh quickly reassured them. 'I don't think we're bothering them,' he said. 'Our boards don't make a noise and they don't have any dangerous parts like propellers. As long as we keep still, the porpoises probably won't even notice us.'

Mandy, James and Josh lay quietly on their boards, keeping a close watch on the porpoise nursery. Mandy kept her fingers crossed in the hope that a calf would reappear and this time for longer. She had only just caught a glimpse of the two little grey shapes that had broken the surface earlier. She'd love to be able to look at their faces.

The only noise that intruded on the tranquil scene was an occasional blow from the pod. It struck Mandy that most people only ever got to see marine mammals in captivity. *And here I am, close enough to touch a group of wild porpoises that are so shy even local people hardly ever see them!* she told herself in amazement.

There was another disturbance among the porpoises. 'What's going on now?' she whispered.

'Perhaps the calves are coming up for air again,' suggested James.

But there was no sign of the youngsters. Instead, the sea around the pod rippled and whirled. It was as if the pod was becoming restless.

'I think they're swimming away,' said Josh.

Disappointed and puzzled, Mandy saw that he was right. The porpoises were moving quickly out to sea. What had made them leave so abruptly? 'Do you think we bothered them?' she asked, as she watched the pod head into the distance using the forward-rolling motion Josh had described. Every now and then, a tiny fin would appear briefly then disappear under the water again. It wasn't long before there was hardly a trace of the little group.

'No,' Josh replied. 'We didn't bother them.' He turned away and stared towards the headland to the right of the bay. 'Something else scared them off,' he said grimly. 'And I think I know just what it was. Listen.'

Mandy and James looked at each other. What was Josh talking about? Mandy listened hard. At first, all she could hear was the sound of the waves washing on to the beach and the distant calls of seagulls soaring above the cliffs. And then, she became aware of a whining noise. It grew louder and louder and was coming their way.

'Blast!' said Josh angrily. 'I *knew* that's what drove them away.'

'What is it?' asked James.

'Jetskis!' Josh blurted out.

As he spoke, about six or seven jetskis rounded the headland. The noisy machines whizzed across the cove, whipping up a swathe of water on all sides. Some of them rode up these large swells, took off into the air and landed with a loud splash before continuing their reckless chase across the cove.

The high-pitched whine of the powerful engines shattered the tranquillity in Sennen Cove. Unlike surfboards which were completely silent, the jetskis caused a huge disturbance. No wonder the porpoises had left so suddenly. Their sensitive sonar systems would have picked up the unnatural noise of the machines long before they rounded the headland.

Mandy now realised why Josh had been so determined to stick to surfing. 'Poor porpoises,' she said, looking sadly out to sea. 'They must have been terrified – especially the little calves. I just hope they can swim fast enough to keep up with the adults.' She bit her lip. It didn't seem fair that the porpoises had been chased out of their own territory.

'The jetskis must be going flat out,' said James, watching them zoom closer.

The rowdy machines were already halfway across the cove and were heading straight for them. Some of the riders were standing up, leaning their bodies from side to side as they bounced through the wakes made by the other jetskis.

'I hope they see us in time!' shouted James above the clamour of the engines.

Mandy nodded. 'We'd better get out of their way,' she cried, as she started to paddle towards the shore.

'Hey!' yelled Josh suddenly. His voice was full of anger. 'There's Ed!'

Shocked, Mandy stopped paddling. She sat up on the surfboard. 'Which one is he?' she called.

Josh pointed to a red jetski at the front of the group. The tall rider in a bright blue wetsuit and black life-jacket waved jauntily as he steered the jetski up the face of a large swell. 'That's him,' Josh said scornfully.

The engine screamed as the jetski roared up the wall of water. At the top of the swell, Ed pulled on the handlebars and the machine became airborne. Mandy was reminded briefly of the way the dolphins had leaped out of the water too. But they had been much more graceful – *and* silent. She heard Ed shout out in triumph. Then he hit the water again, gunned the engine and shot past them with one hand raised in salute.

'Show-off!' shouted Josh.

The spray from Ed's jetski drenched them and their boards rocked up and down on his turbulent wake. Josh was furious. He narrowed his eyes and glared at the back of his departing brother.

Mandy could hardly contain her own anger with the jetski riders. They'd caused a terrible commotion – such a contrast to the peaceful scene only minutes before when the porpoises had been basking so contentedly. 'Do they do this often?' she asked fiercely, staring after the riders.

'Yes, they do,' said Josh, gritting his teeth. 'And it's time they were stopped.'

Three

'We'll probably never get so close to wild porpoises again,' said Mandy, clinging to her surfboard as it bobbed on the waves.

James nodded. 'I wonder if that little pod will ever try to come back here?'

'We can only hope so,' said Josh. He sighed and shook his head. 'I just wish I could make Ed understand what he's doing. I've tried to tell him so many times that he and his friends disturb the marine wildlife in the cove but he just laughs at me and says I'm a killjoy.'

The jetskis were now almost at the far side of

the cove, but the din of their engines still filled the air.

'Doesn't he care about the animals in the cove?' Mandy asked, lying down on the surfboard and starting to paddle back to shore.

'I'm not sure any more,' Josh replied, paddling alongside her. A small swell lifted them and carried the boards along for a short way before it dwindled to become part of the gently rolling ocean again. 'You see, I think all Ed cares about is zooming around as fast as possible.'

Mandy tried to understand. The few rides she'd had on the surfboard that day had certainly been exhilarating. Whizzing across the ocean at top speed must be even more thrilling. But that was no excuse to frighten the wildlife. 'People should consider the animals first,' she said firmly. 'After all, they belong in the sea. We humans are the intruders.'

'I don't think Ed sees it that way,' said Josh wearily. 'He says there's more than enough room in the ocean for everyone. According to him, the porpoises and dolphins can always swim away.'

Mandy didn't like the sound of Ed at all. *He must be a very selfish person*, she thought. She glanced at James, paddling on the other side of her. He pulled a face and Mandy could tell that he didn't think much of Ed either.

In the distance, the jetskis reached the edge of the cove and disappeared round the headland. The whine of the engines grew fainter until, finally, they faded altogether. Almost immediately, Sennen Cove became tranquil again but it was too late for the porpoises. Mandy knew they would be far away by now.

'I'm glad the jetskis have left the cove,' said Josh. 'But it only means they'll be disturbing other animals in the next bay right now.' He looked over his shoulder at an approaching wave and began to paddle hard. 'I think everyone should stick to arm power!' he shouted as the wave came closer.

This time, the wave was strong enough to carry them all the way to the beach. Despite the thrill of the ride, none of them felt like surfing any more. They were all too disheartened by what had happened to the porpoises.

'I'll have to talk to Ed again,' said Josh, as they made their way back through the crowds on the beach to their dry clothes. 'I've *got* to get the message through to him somehow.'

'But if he hasn't listened to you yet,' said Mandy, putting the surfboard down on the sand, 'what makes you think you'll be able to get him to change his mind now?' She picked up her towel and rubbed her short blonde hair. She was sure that Ed was having too much fun on his jetski to be bothered about worrying the local wildlife.

James peeled off his wetsuit and sighed with relief. 'That's better,' he said. He put on his glasses, then turned to Josh. 'Let's suppose Ed *does* listen to you and starts being more careful. How much difference will that make? He isn't the only jetski rider here. What about all the others? How are you going to stop them roaring about the cove?'

Josh hesitated. 'Well . . . I've got an idea from one of my wildlife magazines,' he began. He pulled on a T-shirt. 'In the article I read, someone had started a campaign to protect the marine wildlife on the Scottish coast. I'm going to do the same in Sennen Cove. The person in the article handed out leaflets to people using motorised boats and things, telling them how much damage they can do. I've already written the leaflet I'm going to use. Mum and Dad know all about it,' he added.

'That's great,' said Mandy enthusiastically. She and James had been involved in several similar programmes to help animals in need and knew just how successful such a campaign could be. 'If enough people join in,' she added, 'you could really make a difference. When do you start?'

'Straight away,' said Josh resolutely. 'With Ed. I'm going to tell him just what he and his friends did today.'

As they left the beach, Mandy looked back over her shoulder at the vast Atlantic Ocean. Somewhere in that huge stretch of water was the pod of porpoises. Were they basking contentedly again? Or were they still swimming frantically away, distressed by the jetskis?

The three friends walked along the promenade and through the crowded carparks. Cove Road, which ran along the promenade, was thick with traffic. A car went by, pulling a trailer with a jetski mounted on it. Josh glared at the driver. 'Another one heading for the jetty,' he muttered.

They turned into a narrow lane, then took a

footpath which came out near the Sennen Ice Cream Parlour.

'Why don't we have an ice cream?' suggested James. 'To cheer us up!'

Mandy smiled. 'And if you didn't need cheering up? Would you still want one then?'

James grinned at her. 'I'd think of another reason,' he said. 'Like being on holiday.'

'That's a good enough reason,' Mandy admitted. She realised that she'd been so anxious about the porpoises, she'd almost forgotten that she and James were here to enjoy themselves.

While they waited for the attendant to serve them, they looked at the advertisements on the walls of the parlour.

'Hey! Look at this,' said Mandy, pointing to a colourful poster. 'The Minack Theatre presents the timeless musical *The Wizard of Oz*,' she read aloud. She looked closely at the poster and discovered that the show was being staged every evening that week at the Minack Theatre. Mandy had heard about this famous open-air theatre. Her English teacher at school in Walton had told her class that the stage and seating had been carved out of steep granite cliffs, not far from Sennen

Cove. 'I'd love to see a show there, wouldn't you, James?' Mandy asked.

James didn't seem to hear her. He was too busy watching the attendant scooping ice cream into three cones. Mandy smiled and shook her head. Right now, ice cream was definitely higher on James's list of priorities than a play!

She turned to Josh. 'Have you been to the Minack Theatre?'

'Quite a few times,' said Josh enthusiastically. 'It's really great. Last year we saw *The Three Musketeers* and *The Pirates of Penzance* and a Shakespeare play, *All's Well that Ends Well*. I expect we'll go to a few shows this summer. There's a new show practically every week.'

Expertly devouring his delicious Cornish ice cream, Josh led the way through the narrow lanes and up the hill to the Gills' grey stone house which looked out over the harbour. He showed Mandy and James where to stash the boards, in a shed in the back garden, before they went inside.

'Hi there!' Janet Gill greeted them with a warm smile. She was sorting through a pile of photographs in the living-room. 'Surf good today?'

'Not bad,' said Josh. He ran his hand through his light brown hair and frowned. 'Is Ed home yet?'

'No. I haven't seen him since this morning,' said Janet Gill. 'Why do you want him?'

'To tell him off,' grumbled Josh. 'You won't believe what he and his mates did today.'

'What did they do?' asked Mrs Gill, looking anxiously at Josh.

Josh began to tell her about the porpoises. 'We even spotted two calves . . .'

'But that's wonderful, isn't it?' Janet Gill interrupted. 'Your dad will be so pleased. He's out right now, though. He was called out urgently to Terry George's farm. A heifer with serious mastitis.' She hesitated, suddenly remembering how the conversation had started, then asked, 'But what have the porpoises got to do with Ed and his friends?'

Josh explained how the jetskiers had frightened the porpoises away. 'We were so close to the pod,' he finished sadly. 'Until they were driven away!'

Janet Gill sighed and shook her head. 'I'd hoped Ed would find something other than jetskiing to take his interest by now,' she said. 'I do worry about him.'

'And *I* worry about the dolphins and porpoises!' Josh lashed out.

Janet Gill put her arm round Josh's shoulder. 'I know you do, love,' she said. Then she looked at her watch. 'Your dad should be home soon,' she went on, changing the subject. 'I've got tickets for us all to see *The Wizard of Oz* at the Minack this evening.'

Trying to help lift the atmosphere, Mandy put her worries about the porpoises to one side for the time being. 'Oh, that's brilliant!' she exclaimed. 'We've just been talking about that theatre. I really want to see a show there.'

The others agreed and the uncomfortable moment passed. Mandy, James and Joshua went to shower and change while Janet Gill prepared supper.

During the meal, Chris Gill came in. 'There's one very relieved Friesian heifer at Cliptop Farm right now,' he said as he sat down. 'She calved last week and developed severe mastitis in one teat. She was in a lot of pain, poor thing.'

Mandy listened attentively. 'That means her

milk was clotted, doesn't it?' she asked. Going out on veterinary visits with her mum and dad, she had seen a number of cows suffering from mastitis and knew how painful and serious the condition was.

Chris Gill smiled at her. 'Ah, ever the vet's daughter!' he said in an affectionate voice. 'Yes, Terry and I had to strip the milk from the teat so that I could insert a syringe and give her a shot of strong antibiotic. It should do the trick but I'll call in tomorrow morning to make sure.'

'Will she need treatment with an iodine dip to stop any further infection?' Mandy asked.

Chris Gill looked impressed at Mandy's knowledge. 'Yes, I've told Terry he needs to do that at least twice a day. I hope he'll have the time, though. He's rather busy with calving at the moment.'

As they cleared away the dishes, Josh told his father about their experience with the porpoises and how Ed and his friends had scared them off.

'Well, at least they had the sense to swim out to sea,' said Chris Gill. 'If they'd swum inshore, who knows what might have happened? They could have got stranded.' He put a hand on Josh's shoulder. 'But I agree with you, son. Ed and his friends need to be more aware of marine wildlife. I'll have a word with him.' He turned to Janet Gill. 'Is Ed joining us this evening, Janet?'

'No,' she replied. 'He said he wouldn't be home until quite late tonight. He and his friends are servicing their jetskis.' She looked at Josh sympathetically. 'You're not going to like hearing this,' she said softly. 'They're planning to ride all the way round Land's End tomorrow.'

Josh turned on the sink tap with more force than necessary. 'I've half a mind to sabotage those jetskis,' he burst out angrily.

Janet Gill shook her head. 'An attack like that would make things worse,' she said. 'Ed would never listen to anything you said if you harmed his most prized possession!'

Silently, Mandy agreed. There had to be a better way of making Ed change his attitude.

The Minack Theatre was even more amazing than Mandy had imagined. The whole place seemed to be perched on the side of the cliff. It reminded Mandy of pictures she had seen of ancient open-air theatres in Greece.

The tiered auditorium faced east and south, while, lower down, the stage hung over the sea. Mandy could hear the water lapping on the rocks below. In the distance, on the western horizon, the sea flashed with pink and orange streaks that reflected the shades of the setting sun.

'It's stunning!' Mandy whispered to James as a spotlight lit up the stage. This had to be the most unique theatre she had ever visited – especially as it had such a brilliant view of the sea. 'And with luck, you can watch not only the play but also porpoises and dolphins!' she added, as she lifted her binoculars and scanned the ocean in the background.

The magical setting and the entertaining musical helped Mandy to put aside the problem of the disruptive jetskis for a short time. Even though she had heard the story dozens of times since she was a little girl, Mandy still found herself caught up in the adventures of Dorothy and her dog, Toto, who were carried away by a tornado to the Land of Oz.

As the show progressed, a full moon rose in the clear sky, bathing the amphitheatre in a soft, silver glow. Across the bay, a rocky headland

stood out darkly in the moonlight.

'That's Treryn Dinas,' said Chris Gill during the interval, pointing to the headland. 'It's an Iron Age castle. It always provides a fabulous backdrop to the stage on moonlit nights like this.'

During the second half, Mandy's attention started to wander as thoughts of the porpoises filled her mind. She scanned the sea with her binoculars in the hope of catching a glimpse of a fin or a tail in the bright moonlight. But she knew there was very little chance of spotting anything in the water at night. *I hope they're resting peacefully and that they feel safe again*, she said to herself.

She pictured the two calves they had seen. *I wish they could grow up without being bothered by thoughtless jetski riders*, she thought.

Mandy blinked as the lights in the auditorium were suddenly switched on. The show had come to an end. *Oh well*, she thought, realising that most of the second half had passed her by, *at least I know what the story's all about – thanks to Dad*. She smiled to herself.

She filed out of the row of seats behind the others and joined the throng climbing the slope to the carpark.

'It's certainly one of the best shows I've seen here,' said Janet Gill. 'I thought the Tin Man was particularly good,' she added. 'That costume was very realistic!'

'I bet I know who Mandy liked the best,' said James with a smile. 'Either the lion or Toto the dog!'

'Is that right, Mandy?' asked Janet Gill.

Mandy nodded. But real-life animals were occupying her thoughts much more than characters on a stage. She hoped no one had seen her staring out to sea for most of the play – especially as she'd been so keen on coming to the theatre in the first place.

'It's a pity Ed didn't come with us,' said Chris Gill. 'He'd have enjoyed it too.'

Josh looked at his father and grimaced. 'Come off it, Dad! You don't really believe that, do you? You know Ed's not interested in anything but his terrible jetski,' he said tightly.

Chris Gill sighed. 'We can always hope,' he said.

Josh nodded.

But Mandy could see that he was still smarting over the incident that afternoon with his brother and the other jetskiers. If what Josh had told them about Ed was anything to go by, it looked like it was going to take a miracle to make Ed change his attitude. Not just wishful thinking.

Four

Mandy could hardly believe she was still in Sennen Cove when she woke the next morning. Outside, a howling wind was buffeting the house, making the window panes rattle in their frames. She pulled on her jeans and a sweater and joined the others for breakfast.

From the kitchen window, Mandy could see the fishing boats rocking and swaying on the choppy water in the small harbour below. Enormous waves crashed against the long stone wall that surrounded the moorings, shooting great spumes of spray over the boats. Fishermen in bright yellow oilskins battled against the gale to secure their boats.

'What a change from yesterday,' said Mandy, staring out of the window. She could still picture the bright sun and the calm sea of the day before.

'It certainly is a big contrast,' agreed Chris Gill, pouring himself a cup of coffee. 'But we're quite used to storms like this down here.'

'I hope it blows over soon,' said James, buttering a slice of toast. 'I want to get back on the boogie-board!'

Josh grinned at him. 'It sounds like you're getting the surfing bug too!' he said. He stood next to Mandy at the window and looked across to Whitesands Bay. Even from a distance, they could see the huge waves pounding the shore. 'Some surfers have the bug so badly that they even go out on days like this,' said Josh.

Mandy grimaced. 'You'd have to be really crazy to do that,' she said.

Just then, Ed came in. 'Morning everyone,' he yawned, pouring a glass of orange juice which he gulped down in one go.

Apart from their brief encounter with him in the sea yesterday, this was the first time Mandy and James had actually met Ed. When they'd returned from the theatre late the previous night, he hadn't yet come home.

'This is Ed,' Josh muttered reluctantly.

'Hi,' said Mandy, a little warily, as she sat down at the table.

Ed smiled at her. 'Hi,' he said. 'Sorry I haven't been around much. Busy time – the holidays!' He looked at his watch. 'Hmm! I have to run. Everyone's waiting for me at the jetty.' He grabbed an apple and headed for the door. 'We've got some great action planned.'

'Wait!' called Josh. 'I've got to talk to you.'

'Sorry,' came Ed's voice from the hallway. 'It'll have to wait.'

'It can't wait,' Josh shouted after him. 'You've got to stop worrying the porpoises.'

'Worrying the porpoises?' echoed Ed. 'We don't go anywhere near them.'

'You did yesterday,' insisted Josh. 'There was a whole nursery of harbour porpoises in the bay and you and your mates scared them off.' But it was too late. Ed was slamming the front door behind him as Josh spoke.

Josh sighed in frustration. 'Why won't he listen

to me?' he said angrily, his face red with rage.

Janet Gill tried to console him. 'Let's just be glad that the porpoises can outswim the jetskis,' she said.

'That's not the point,' Josh muttered. 'They shouldn't *have* to run away to be safe.'

Chris Gill stood up. 'I agree with you, Josh,' he said. 'The porpoises should be entitled to a safe environment. Who knows what damage humans cause when we invade their territory? Jetskiers are probably responsible for more than they realise.' He looked seriously at his younger son. 'I'll try to reason with Ed when he comes home.' Then, taking his raincoat from the back of his chair, he said, 'If that doesn't work then we ought to try targeting others with this leaflet campaign. Still, let's look on the bright side of things. The storm might help in one way.'

'How?' asked James.

'It might have driven any marine mammals far out to sea by now, which means Ed and his pals won't be able to cause them any distress today,' Mr Gill explained. He picked up his car keys from the sideboard. 'Well, time to do my rounds,' he said. 'Storm or no storm, there are always land mammals to see to!'

Mandy, James and Josh sat gloomily round the table. Mandy hoped Chris Gill was right in thinking that the porpoises would be well out to sea by the time the jetskis took to the water. But what if they weren't?

Janet Gill stood with her back to the window, frowning at their long faces. 'Try not to feel too miserable,' she said. 'I'm sure that things will be all right.'

Josh shrugged. Mandy could see he didn't share his mother's confidence.

'Why don't you take your cameras and go down to the beach?' Janet Gill suggested. 'It might take your mind off things and there could be some fantastic photo opportunities down there in this storm. I may even go out myself later today.'

'That's a good idea,' said Mandy, looking at Josh and James who nodded their approval.

'If you get any good shots, we'll develop them later,' Mrs Gill promised.

'Thanks.' Mandy looked pleased.

It was useful that Janet Gill had her own darkroom for developing photographs, but not that surprising. She was well known in the area for her photography and had won several competition prizes.

Mandy, James and Joshua fetched their cameras. 'I'll bring my binoculars, too,' said Mandy, slinging them round her neck.

When she felt the full force of the gale outside, Mandy wondered if Ed and his friends would reconsider their plans to ride along the coast. She could hear the huge waves thundering against the granite rocks in the cove. Even though the jetskis' engines were powerful, surely Ed and the others would find the conditions too dangerous?

Leaning into the wind, Mandy followed James and Joshua out of the relàtive shelter of the Gill's garden and on to the narrow lane behind the house.

'We'll go a different way today,' said Josh. 'Along the footpath that goes through Terry George's land. His farm is on top of the cliffs. You can see the whole cove from there.'

The footpath took them through lush pastures and past a herd of Friesian cattle filing solemnly out of a milking shed. The cows shuffled restlessly and mooed as they passed, eager to get back to their field.

Seeing them, Mandy remembered the sick cow Chris Gill had been treating. 'I wonder how the heifer is?' she said to Josh. 'Do you think we can go and see her?'

Josh led them round the side of the shed. 'Dad's here so I don't see why not,' he said, seeing his father's car parked in the driveway outside the stone farmhouse. He pointed to a nearby barn. 'He's probably in there,' he said.

Josh led the way across the yard, closely followed by Mandy and James. He pushed back the door to the barn. Inside it was dark and silent. It was a relief to be out of the buffeting wind. At the far end, Chris Gill and Terry George were standing next to a pen which held the heifer and her calf. Mr George was short and wiry with a craggy, sunburnt face and big, calloused hands. He was definitely a man who spent most of his life outdoors, and reminded Mandy of the hill farmers who lived near Welford.

'Well, look who's here,' said Chris Gill when he saw the three friends coming towards him. 'Not surfing today?' he joked.

'Not yet,' James said, grinning. 'We're waiting for the waves to get bigger!'

'And the wind to become a tornado,' joined in Josh.

'Let me know when that happens and I'll join you.' Chris Gill laughed.

Mandy leaned over the railings and gently stroked the little calf that was suckling from his mother. His black-and-white coat was as soft and smooth as velvet. He couldn't have been more than a few days old.

The little animal stopped nursing for a moment. He turned and focused his limpid brown eyes on Mandy. She stretched her hand out to him and he sniffed at it. 'You're beautiful,' she said, smiling as his damp, shiny nose blew little puffs of hot air on her fingers.

Mandy rubbed his cheeks gently, then straightened up and looked at the heifer. 'Is she any better today?' she asked Chris Gill.

'Yes, the inflammation has gone down a bit and she's not in quite so much pain,' he told her. 'But she'll have to stay inside for a few more days for the iodine treatment.'

'That'll keep me on my toes,' said Terry George.

'What with the calving and now this, I'll be lucky to get any sleep! I could do with an extra farmhand or two.'

'I'll help you,' Mandy blurted out automatically. She could never pass up an opportunity to help an animal.

Terry George looked at her, surprised.

'I'd be happy to come and do the iodine dip once or twice a day,' Mandy went on.

The farmer frowned. 'Well, I don't know if . . .'

'You don't have to worry, Terry,' interrupted Chris Gill. 'Mandy knows exactly what to do. Her father's also a vet. He's a good friend of mine. Mandy's been around sick animals all her life, and she probably knows as much, if not more, than the average first-year student at veterinary college!'

Mandy smiled shyly at the compliment. It was true that she knew more than most people her age but she also knew that there would always be more to learn.

James agreed with Chris Gill. 'There's your chance, Mandy,' he added. 'Seeing as you're ready for college, you can just skip secondary school!'

'Sounds good,' Mandy said with a grin. 'Then I

can become the youngest vet in the world!'

'Well, you can start by serving part of your apprenticeship here,' offered Terry George. He handed Mandy a plastic beaker filled with thick yellow iodine.

Mandy crouched down and slid the beaker over the affected teat. She had to hold it firmly because the calf kept nudging it inquisitively. 'That should do for now,' she said after a few moments. She gently pushed the nuzzling calf away. 'And don't you lick this teat too much,' she said to the young animal. 'We don't want it getting dirty and being infected again.'

Grateful for Mandy's readiness to help, Terry George invited them all in for a hot drink. 'I know my wife was baking yesterday!' he added.

'Yes, please!' said James, jumping at the chance to sample some fresh Cornish cakes and pastries.

But at the same time that James spoke, Mandy and Josh declined the offer. They were both very eager to go down to the beach.

James grinned and shrugged his shoulders. 'Out-voted again,' he said good-naturedly, as they left the barn.

Terry George's land extended to the cliffs

overlooking the bay. In single file, they battled their way through the wind, then stood on the cliff top and looked out at the raging sea, which foamed and swirled as far as the eye could see.

'This should make a good picture,' said Mandy, preparing to snap the turbulent scene. But as she steadied the camera, she noticed something else in the viewfinder. At the same time, she became aware of a now-familiar, unpleasant sound. 'Jetskis!' she exclaimed, lowering the camera and staring aghast as a group of them shot noisily through the heaving sea. Even the howling wind couldn't block out the relentless whine of the engines.

Mandy peered through her binoculars. 'I think I can see Ed,' she said after a while. She passed the binoculars to Josh. 'Now I know for sure he's crazy!' she added sombrely.

Josh stared grimly at the rowdy fleet, then handed the binoculars back to Mandy. Heaving a big sigh, he shook his head in despair before heading for a narrow path, which led down the granite cliffs to a secluded rocky beach.

At the bottom of the cliff, they were able to appreciate just how big the waves were.

'They're like mountains!' exclaimed James, staring at the gigantic grey rollers pounding the shore. 'It's really awesome. I wish I had a video camera.'

The tide was so high that the beach was almost completely submerged. Only the largest rocks and a narrow strip of gravelly sand at the base of the cliffs escaped the drenching waves.

Mandy looked up and down the windswept beach. It was deserted except for a few hardy seagulls which strutted about looking for tasty morsels among the rocks. She followed Joshua and James as they picked their way along the dry strip of sand, clambering over large rocks and leaping across tidal pools, filled by the heavy sea.

When they came to a particularly big rock, James asked Mandy and Josh to stand on top of it with their backs to the sea. 'With the stormy water behind you, it will make a really good picture,' he said. As James pressed the button, a huge wave crashed in the background, sending a flume of spray spewing over the rock. Mandy and Josh were drenched!

James roared with laughter. 'Now I *really* wish I had a video camera,' he joked.

James couldn't resist taking another shot of his bedraggled friends and didn't notice a wide swathe of water swooping up to where he was standing. In seconds, he was up to his knees in water!

'Now we're even!' called Mandy, quickly taking a snap of James before the wave receded.

Mandy saw that Josh was grinning broadly. It was just what he needed to cheer him up a little, after the unwelcome sight of the jetskis. 'Those will be brilliant pictures! I can't wait to see them,' he said, laughing.

They continued along the beach, hugging the bottom of the cliffs to avoid another soaking. James noticed some nests perched precariously on the cliff-face.

'Let's have a look at those,' he suggested. He and Josh started clambering up the rocks to identify which birds had made the nests.

Mandy went ahead, preferring to explore the rocks. The tide was starting to go out now so the high-water line was clearly visible on the sandy parts of the beach. Among the rocks were pools of water that had been left behind by the raging sea. In the pools, tiny fish darted about, trapped until the next high tide came to wash them out to sea again.

A seagull posed on top of a huge stretch of rock which rose out of the sand just ahead of Mandy, blocking her path. She lifted her camera to take a shot of the bird. As the shutter clicked, Mandy thought she heard a sneeze. She held her breath and listened. Above the racket of the storm, she made out another distinctive sneezing sound. It reminded her of the porpoise blow she had heard yesterday. The sneeze seemed to have come from behind the ridge of granite just ahead. *I wonder if someone's sheltering behind there?* Mandy thought, going towards it.

The seagull took off, shrieking indignantly, as Mandy neared the rocks. 'Sorry to disturb you,' she said, grinning as she clambered up the jagged boulders.

Mandy peered over the top of the rock, and gasped.

Lying motionless beneath the water, in a large rock pool below her, was the dark grey form of a porpoise.

Five

Mandy slithered down the rock towards the pool. 'What happened to you?' she whispered breathlessly. She lay down on her stomach so that she could get a closer look at the creature without alarming it. She knew not to get too near; the porpoise could be injured and shocked, and Mandy's presence would only add to the trauma it was suffering.

The porpoise was about a metre in length and its small dorsal fin was just visible at the surface. Mandy guessed that it was still quite young – too young, probably, to be away from its mother. How had it come to be trapped in the pool? 'Why are you all alone?' she asked quietly. From what she'd seen yesterday, porpoises kept close together even when they were moving through the water.

Mandy bit her lip as a thought came to her. The jetskis! Were they somehow responsible for this?

There was a ripple in the pool. The porpoise's back broke the surface of the water momentarily and there came the sharp blow that was now so familiar to Mandy. And then, quite unexpectedly, the porpoise lifted its head and looked straight at Mandy.

Mandy's heart skipped a beat as she found herself staring into its intelligent but sad-looking eyes. 'I'll get help for you, I promise,' she said gently.

Silently, the porpoise dipped its head back under the water.

Mandy scrambled to her feet and climbed back to the top of the rock. She looked around for James and Joshua. They were still clambering along the rocks at the bottom of the cliffs. She beckoned to them urgently.

'Found something interesting?' called James as

he climbed up the granite ridge.

'A porpoise,' whispered Mandy when they had reached her.

James and Josh looked at her disbelievingly.

But when they reached the top of the rock and peered down into the pool, their disbelief changed to deep concern.

'Oh no!' exclaimed James. 'How did it get there?'

For a minute Joshua was speechless as he stared, wide-eyed, at the porpoise. Then, through clenched teeth, he hissed, 'Ed and his mates. I bet they're responsible for this!'

'How can you be sure it was their fault?' asked James. He took off his glasses and wiped away a film of sticky sea salt that was coating them.

'Because it's too much of a coincidence that they went roaring past just now,' said Josh.

'We'll probably never know the truth,' said Mandy hastily. 'Surely the important thing now is to get some help.'

'You're right,' said Josh. 'And the best person for that is my dad. He'll know exactly what to do. He went on a course about stranded marine mammals a couple of years ago and he's already had lots of experience with beached dolphins. I'll go and fetch him.' He glanced up at the cliff top. 'Let's hope he's still with Terry George,' he said. He leaped off the rock on to a patch of sand. Then, without a backward glance, he tore off towards the farm.

Below, in its watery prison, the little porpoise was growing restless. Breaking the surface once or twice, it began to move about in the pool.

'I think it's trying to find a way out,' said Mandy.

The porpoise swam the few metres to one end of the pool then, finding its way blocked by a rocky wall, turned and swam to the other end.

James grimaced. 'It's hurt,' he said, anxiously. 'Look at the cuts and grazes on its sides.'

Mandy's eyes widened in shock. 'They look really sore. I suppose they were caused by the sharp rocks.' She imagined the little creature being battered about by the huge waves. 'I hope Mr Gill will be able to treat it,' she added, biting her thumbnail.

The porpoise reached the jagged seaward side of the pool and lifted its head briefly as if it was trying to look over the edge. Then it began to swim in tight circles round the pool.

'Poor little porpoise,' murmured Mandy. 'It's in so much distress. If only we could do something to calm it down until Chris arrives.' She ached to stroke it but she knew that only a qualified person like Josh's father should handle the porpoise. The last thing Mandy wanted to do was to cause it even more stress.

James seemed lost in thought. He stared out to sea, his face creased in a frown. Then he suddenly clicked his fingers. 'Wait a minute,' he said softly. 'There *is* something we can do while we're waiting.'

Mandy gave him a questioning look. Sometimes, James had some really good ideas. But what was he going to suggest this time? It wasn't going to be easy to soothe a distressed, trapped porpoise.

'We can sing to the porpoise,' James told her.

'Sing to it?' Mandy echoed, puzzled.

'Uh-huh,' said James, nodding his head earnestly. 'I read that on the Internet. They say it really works.'

Mandy grinned at him. James was as crazy about computers as he was about animals.

'You see, when I heard we were coming down

to Cornwall, I checked out some web sites on marine mammals. On one of the sites, there was something about how rescuers often talk and sing to beached whales, dolphins and porpoises to calm them until they can be refloated,' James explained.

This made sense to Mandy. She had heard recordings of the haunting calls of some marine mammals. She knew that the echoing cries travelled for long distances and could be heard by other whales many miles away. She nodded. 'It's worth a go, James. Good thinking,' she said, smiling.

'I didn't have to think too hard,' James replied. 'Thank the Internet!'

Mandy couldn't resist teasing James a little. 'It's a pity you're not as good at sea surfing as you are at cyber surfing!' she sighed.

James made a face at her. 'You just wait,' he said, laughing. 'I just need to get some practice in. Then we'll see who's the ace surfer!'

The porpoise continued to swim about restlessly. Being careful not to make any sudden movements, Mandy and James lay on their stomachs on the rock.

'What shall we sing?' James asked.

'I don't know,' Mandy replied. 'But I would guess it needs to be something fairly tuneful.'

'What about something we heard in the play last night?' suggested James. 'Like "Over the Rainbow". I bet you know all the words from when you were little!'

'I do,' Mandy admitted with a grin. 'But I think we should change the words to suit the porpoise.'

'OK,' said James, and they began to hum quietly to the porpoise.

'Somewhere over the seashore,' sang Mandy. She turned and grinned at James, then carried on.

'I think it's working,' whispered Mandy, after about ten minutes.

The little creature was no longer swimming round in agitation and was floating in the water just below Mandy and James.

Mandy felt a glimmer of hope. She tried to convince herself that if the porpoise came to no more harm, there was a chance it could recover and be returned safely to the ocean. She had been involved in a similar operation before and knew that it was possible.

When she was in Florida, Mandy had helped with a successful campaign to return a captive, performing dolphin to the ocean. She would never forget the wonderful sight of Bing, the bottlenose dolphin, swimming out to sea to join a group of wild dolphins that were waiting for him. 'We'll do everything we can to make sure you'll soon be doing the same, little one,' Mandy murmured to the porpoise.

By now, the wind had begun to subside and the tide was much lower. Only a few minutes before, the water had come up as far as the pool, but now there was a strip of dry sand between it and the sea. Despite the calmer conditions, Mandy felt a niggling concern. The low tide meant that the porpoise was now well and truly stranded in the rock pool. The patch of beach between the pool and the ocean was growing wider all the time. Soon the little animal would be a long way from its usual home.

But at least the porpoise was in water and not on dry land. Mandy knew that on dry land it would be in danger of overheating and sunburn, even in cooler weather.

'I wonder if I should take a photograph of it?'

said James, hesitantly lifting his camera.

'I suppose if we keep well back we could take one or two shots without frightening it,' said Mandy.

Slowly she focused her camera on the porpoise. Next to her, she heard the shutter clicking on James's camera. And at that very instant, the porpoise lifted her head clear out of the water and looked up at them briefly – at exactly the moment that Mandy pressed the button on her

camera! 'I think I've got a shot of its face!' she breathed, almost unable to believe her luck.

'I hope so,' said James. 'I was just a second too early.'

It seemed an age before Joshua returned with his father and Terry George. Mandy felt a huge surge of relief as she watched Chris Gill and Mr George climbing cautiously round to the front of the rock pool. The ledge of the pool was at waist height to the men, which meant they could watch the porpoise without disturbing it too much.

Mandy clambered down and joined the others on the ground. Chris Gill pulled himself up on to the rocky ledge and looked closely at the porpoise.

'Pass me my bag, someone, please,' he whispered over his shoulder.

Mandy reached for Chris Gill's bulky veterinary bag, which he'd left on the sand. She held it up to him.

'I think I could do with a bit of help,' said Mr Gill, taking the bag and pulling Mandy up on to the ledge at the same time.

Cautiously, Mandy kneeled next to Chris Gill at the poolside. Now she was only a couple of metres from the porpoise. 'Is it going to be all right?' she asked Mr Gill anxiously.

Joshua's dad shrugged his shoulders. 'It's hard to say,' he said grimly. 'Those skin grazes look quite nasty but the biggest danger is going to be shock. It's common for beached marine mammals to die from shock before we do anything to help them.' He reached into his bag for a syringe. 'I'll give it a shot of long-acting antibiotic to hold off any infection and apply some waterproof antiseptic ointment to those wounds,' he said. He looked at Mandy and shook his head. 'I can treat the cuts but shock is a different matter altogether. To tell you the truth, I don't hold out much hope for this porpoise.'

Mandy's heart lurched. There had to be *something* they could do.

Chris Gill skilfully caught hold of the porpoise, then gently injected the antibiotic. 'Pass me the ointment,' he said to Mandy, handing her the used syringe.

Mandy gave Josh's dad the tube and watched while he carefully applied the antiseptic cream to the larger cuts on the porpoise's smooth grey body. When he had finished, he let go of the porpoise and it swam nervously out of his reach.

'I think that's enough close contact for now,' the vet said, sitting back on his heels. 'We don't want to make matters worse.'

They eased themselves off the ledge and on to the ground.

'What do you think happened to it, Chris?' asked Terry George.

'It's difficult to say,' Chris Gill answered. 'There are all sorts of reasons for marine mammals getting stranded but it's my guess the storm played a big role in this.' He looked out to sea. 'This little one was probably terrified by the surging seas and became disorientated.'

'I think it was more than that,' Josh blurted out. 'I bet the jetskis are the main culprits!'

Chris Gill nodded. 'Could be,' he said. 'If the porpoise was already frightened by the storm, the jetskis could have made it panic and then lose the rest of its group.'

Josh took a deep breath. 'Just wait until I get hold of Ed this time,' he muttered.

'I think we should concentrate on doing what we can for the porpoise,' said Mandy, trying to calm Josh down. Despite Chris Gill's gloomy predictions about its chances of survival, Mandy still wanted to believe the porpoise could be saved. 'Why don't we think up a name?' she suggested. 'We can't just keep saying "it".'

James and Josh nodded.

'The trouble is, we don't know whether it's a male or female,' said James. 'Is there any way of telling?' he asked Josh's dad.

'I'm fairly sure it's a female,' said Chris Gill. 'It's not easy to tell but I'm sure I noticed two mammary slits while I was giving her the injection.'

Everyone gazed at the porpoise, trying to think of a suitable name for her.

'How about Storm?' suggested James.

'That's OK,' said Mandy, hesitantly. 'But I think she's too gentle-looking to be named after something so destructive.' In her mind, she saw once more the beseeching look in the creature's eyes. 'She reminds me of something calm and beautiful,' she said. 'Almost like a mermaid resting in a rockpool.'

'Then let's call her Morveren,' said Josh. 'It's Cornish for mermaid,' he explained.

'Morveren,' echoed Mandy. 'That's perfect!'

Six

'What do we do next?' Mandy asked Josh's dad, as she watched him close up his veterinary bag.

'Not much, I'm afraid,' said Chris Gill. 'All we can do now is wait. The wounds will heal in time – porpoises and dolphins have quite tough skin. But the important thing is for her to get over the shock. We'll have to try and get her to eat, of course, although she may be too shocked to take any food. Then, assuming she does survive, we'll have to refloat her as soon as possible.'

Mandy stared at the motionless form of the porpoise. 'You *will* survive, won't you, Morveren?'

she said firmly but, at the back of her mind, she knew she was just trying to convince herself that everything would be all right. Then, turning to Chris Gill she asked, 'How will we get her back into the sea?'

'It's a bit early to start thinking along those lines,' Mr Gill told her. 'We'll have to see how she does first but in this situation we would wait for the tide to come back in and hope she'd be able to make her own way out of the rock pool.' He looked out to sea. 'The trouble is, the water isn't likely to rise quite so high again at this time of year. The storm caused an unusually big tide.'

'Couldn't we stretcher her out?' suggested Josh. 'Like we've done with beached dolphins before?'

'Mmm. That would be our only alternative,' said his dad. 'But it's not an ideal solution, as we want to avoid handling her any more than we have to.'

'It might not come to that,' said Terry George.

Mandy looked at him hopefully.

The farmer went on. 'You see, I've just heard the long-range weather forecast and they say there's another big storm on the way. It should reach us in a day or two. If it's as big as this morning's storm, it should push the water all the way up here again,' he said.

This was encouraging news and, for once, Mandy found herself wishing for bad weather! She looked across the sea to the southern horizon. The sky was growing clearer and even had some patches of blue in it. The wind had dropped so that there were now only a few white horses cresting the waves. It didn't seem possible that another raging storm was on the way. 'I hope the weather people are right,' she said doubtfully.

'So do I,' said Chris Gill. 'Assuming Morveren does survive her time in the pool, it really would be best for her to find her own way out. The less she is handled, the better. Unnecessary touching would simply cause her more stress.' He took his bag from the rocky ledge. 'I really ought to go,' he said. 'The surgery is probably rather crowded by now!'

He turned to Mandy, James and Joshua. 'You three will have to keep a watch on Morveren. We don't want anyone else chancing upon her. If word spreads about a stranded porpoise, it would be disastrous. People would come from miles around to have a look at her.'

Mandy understood that Morveren would be dangerously stressed if she was surrounded by crowds of onlookers. 'If only we could stop people from coming to this beach,' she said.

'Fortunately, people don't often come here,' Terry George reassured her. 'It's a fairly inaccessible spot unless you go through my farm,' he explained. 'But, to be on the safe side, why don't you three set up a beach camp? You could spend the night here and take it in turns to keep watch over Morveren. If there are any problems, you can always run up to us at the farm.'

He looked at Mandy and winked. 'And of course, it's not too far for you to come up and check on the heifer for me! You haven't forgotten about her in all the drama of Morveren, have you?'

Mandy smiled at him. 'No. She was just at the back of my mind for a while. But of course I'll still come up to see to her,' she reassured the farmer.

'Right, that's decided then,' said Chris Gill, walking away from the rock pool. 'You're going to have to pitch a tent for yourselves, but more importantly, we'll need to get some food for Morveren,' he told them. 'I suggest two of you come back with me now. We'll go and buy some fresh fish at the village shop. If you drop it in the pool, she may just be tempted to take it.'

'You'll be lucky to get any, I reckon,' said Terry George. 'The storm will probably have kept the fishing boats from going out today.'

'Mmm. You have a point there,' replied Chris Gill, stopping for a moment. 'But let's hope for the best.' He turned to Mandy. 'I may not able to get down to check on Morveren again until later tomorrow. So you three are on your own in this.'

'That's OK,' said Mandy. She was used to the responsibility of caring for an injured animal on her own. 'And I'm quite happy to stay here with Morveren now while Josh and James fetch the fish.'

'We'll try to find a tent as well,' said Josh, starting out behind his father.

'And some food for us?' asked James hopefully.

Mandy couldn't help laughing. James always made sure he wouldn't starve.

'I can help you out there,' said Terry George. 'You can have fresh milk, homemade bread, apples from my orchard – whatever you need. Mandy can pick it up when she's seeing to the heifer.'

'Terrific!' James grinned as he set off with Josh and the two men.

After the others had gone, Mandy stood with her elbows resting on the rocky ledge at the front of the pool and watched Morveren. She hummed quietly from time to time, feeling very privileged to be all alone with a rare harbour porpoise. *And so close too*, Mandy told herself. *Even closer than I was to the group in the sea yesterday.*

It didn't seem long before James and Joshua returned, staggering under the weight of loaded rucksacks. Mandy was amazed at what they'd brought back with them. Janet Gill had sorted out a change of clothing for each of them, toothbrushes and toothpaste and three sleeping bags. But most importantly, they also had supplies for Morveren. Not only did Joshua have a cool box full of freshly caught fish but James was gripping the handle of a bucket that was brimming over with fish scraps.

'You won't believe this,' said Josh, 'but Ed found these scraps for us!'

'I *don't* believe you,' said Mandy, shaking her head.

'It's true,' said James. 'We met him in the village.

He was on his way back from Land's End. Josh told him about Morveren and how it was his fault that she's stranded.'

'What did Ed say?' asked Mandy, taking a handful of fish out of the bucket. She grimaced and turned her face away. It smelled horrible! Still, she'd have to put up with the fishy stench. Morveren needed to eat.

'He didn't say a thing at first,' James told her. 'He just stormed away from us!'

'So we couldn't believe our eyes when we were in the village shop and he came in with this bucket of scraps,' went on Josh. 'He said he'd been down to the harbour and asked Mr MacDonald – the man Ed works for – to give them to him. I was really glad because what with the storm, the shop didn't have a lot of fish.'

Mandy was astonished. But she was in for another surprise.

'You're not going to believe this either,' said Josh, holding up a bulky canvas bag. 'Ed lent us his tent when I told him we were staying here to keep a watch on Morveren.'

Mandy shook her head in disbelief. Was it possible that Ed was feeling guilty for disturbing the porpoises? Perhaps he cared more for the marine wildlife than he was prepared to admit.

She went over to the pool. 'I really hope she'll eat,' said Mandy, dropping the fish scraps into the water. 'That will show that she's not too stressed.'

James and Josh followed her, carrying the rest of the fish. They stood beside the rocky ledge, quietly watching the little porpoise.

'I don't think she's very interested,' said James, disappointed.

The fish pieces floated round the pool but Morveren didn't even look at them. A cheeky seagull saw his opportunity and swooped down to grab a fish tail.

'Well, at least it's not going to waste,' James observed, as the seagull settled on a nearby rock and swallowed the food.

'Mmm,' murmured Mandy. 'But we don't want to be feeding too many gulls. There'll be hundreds of them here in a flash if they get a whiff of the fish.' She thought of how fishing boats coming into harbour were always surrounded by flocks of seagulls hoping to grab a morsel or two.

'Let's try a whole fish,' said Joshua. He opened the cool box and took out one of the fish they'd bought from the fishmonger. But just as he was about to put it in the pool, Morveren turned her head and reluctantly took one of the scraps floating about the pool.

'Good girl!' whispered Mandy happily. 'Now take another one.'

But Morveren ignored the rest of the fish – even the whole one that Josh slipped into the water.

'I don't think she's got much of an appetite,' said James. 'Not like me, at any rate!'

'You take some beating when it comes to that,' Mandy joked. Then, more seriously, she added, 'I guess Morveren's feeling too shocked and frightened to eat very much. Still, at least she did eat something. That must be a good sign. Let's try again later.'

'In the meantime, we can look for a good place to pitch the tent,' suggested Josh.

They settled on a flat sandy patch, sheltered on two sides by large rocks, not far from Morveren's pool. 'If another storm's on the way, we'll want to be out of the wind,' said Josh, pulling the tent out of its bag and tipping the tent pegs on to the sand.

Soon their dark green shelter stood snugly between the rocks.

'Now all we need is some food,' said James.

Mandy looked at her watch. A long time had passed since Terry George's cow had last been treated. 'I'll go up to the farm to see to the heifer,' she told the others. 'And I'll bring back the food Mr George promised us.'

James's face broke into an appreciative grin. 'I was hoping you'd say that,' he said.

Mandy was reluctant to leave Morveren, but at the same time she didn't want to let Mr George or the heifer down. Besides, she was able to help the heifer whereas there wasn't much she could do right now for Morveren other than keeping an eye on her. With James and Joshua on the beach, Morveren would be well protected.

Terry George was in the barn when Mandy arrived at the farm. 'Thank goodness you're here, lass,' he called from a corner pen as she entered. 'I've got my hands full with two calvings right now. I can't spare a moment for the heifer.'

'Don't worry about her,' said Mandy. 'I

promised you I'd come twice a day and I will.'

'Chris Gill said I could rely on you,' Terry George said gratefully. 'Oh, and don't forget – there's a picnic hamper for you and your friends in the kitchen.'

'Thank you very much,' said Mandy. 'I'll pick it up on my way back.' She hurried to the heifer's pen. The tiny calf seemed to recognise her because it came straight over and nudged her hand. Mandy rubbed its velvety nose. 'I hope you're not pushing this against your poor mother's sore teat,' she said.

The calf gave a high-pitched moo and nudged Mandy's legs as Mandy turned away and reached for the iodine bottle on a shelf above the pen.

'I haven't come here to pet you,' Mandy said, smiling. She poured some of the dark yellow fluid into a beaker and held it over the affected teat. The heifer gazed at Mandy dolefully. Mandy rubbed her side gently. 'I know you've had a hard time.' Mandy spoke soothingly. 'But you'll soon be fine and then you can go back in the fields with the rest of the herd.'

As soon as Mandy had finished, the calf snuggled against her mother and began to suckle.

'That's good,' Mandy murmured. The calf had to keep drinking otherwise the heifer would feel very uncomfortable from all the milk inside her. 'But keep away from the sore teat,' Mandy instructed. She watched the calf feeding hungrily for a few minutes. *I wish Morveren was that eager to feed,* Mandy thought, replacing the iodine and beaker on the shelf.

On her way out of the barn, she stopped briefly

to see how the calving was progressing.

'Very slowly,' said Terry George in answer to Mandy's question. He patted the rump of a heavily pregnant cow. 'But it shouldn't be long now before this one's calf arrives.'

Mandy told Mr George she would return the next morning.

'Then you can meet the brand new members of the herd,' he said.

'That'll be great,' Mandy replied. 'I adore newborn calves.'

'It seems to me you adore all animals.' Terry George chuckled.

'So far I do,' Mandy agreed. 'I haven't met an animal yet that I don't like. Perhaps I wouldn't be too keen on a scorpion or tarantula though!' she joked.

'That seems a bit unfair,' teased Mr George. 'Just because they're deadly poisonous and don't look at you with big brown eyes like porpoises and calves doesn't mean you have to turn your back on them.'

Mandy laughed. 'I don't think I'd ever turn my back on a scorpion or a tarantula. I would want to see exactly where they were and if they were coming after me!' she said as she left the barn.

In the farmhouse, an enormous picnic basket was standing on the kitchen table. It was overflowing with homemade bread, pies and cakes and freshly picked fruit. *James will be in his element!* Mandy thought and grinned to herself. She wondered if Mrs George was around so that she could thank her, but there was no sign of the farmer's wife.

She's probably busy as well, Mandy decided. *I'll thank her another time.* She was eager to return to Morveren and see if the porpoise had taken any more food. *And I suppose James is just as eager for me to return with our rations!* she thought with a smile as she ran across the field to the cliff path.

Seven

'Let's toast some marshmallows,' Mandy said, as the three friends sat round their campfire that evening.

'Do you mean there are marshmallows too?' asked James in surprise.

'Uh-huh.' Mandy grinned, taking a packet of them out of the picnic basket. 'Mr and Mrs George thought of everything!'

The basket had contained a wonderful picnic. And the beach had provided them with a perfect picnic spot. Searching among the cliffs, they had found some dry pieces of driftwood, washed up in nooks and crannies. Mrs George must have guessed they'd want to make a fire because she had included a box of matches with the food.

'We need something for holding the marshmallows in the flames,' said Mandy.

'This should do the trick,' said Josh, pulling a skewer out of the basket. 'We can thread the marshmallows on to it.'

'Great,' Mandy said.

'Marshmallow kebabs for pudding,' remarked James, pushing the sweets on to the skewer.

It was a tranquil, moonlit night. The wind had dropped completely and the water was so calm that it lapped gently on the shore, barely making a sound. It was hard to believe there had been such a violent storm only hours before. Apart from the hushed whoosh of the water, the only other noise on the beach was an occasional sharp *choo* from Morveren in the rockpool.

The little porpoise had eaten another piece of fish since Mandy's return from the farm but since then had refused to take any more. Mandy hoped that, once night fell, Morveren would become more relaxed, and then she would eat the rest of the fish floating in the pool.

In contrast to Morveren's reluctance to eat, James was tucking enthusiastically into the marshmallows. 'They're delicious,' he said, pulling another one off the wire. 'The best I've ever had.' He had wrapped a piece of kitchen towel round one end of the skewer so that he wouldn't burn himself on the hot metal.

'Maybe that's because we're beside the sea,' suggested Joshua, also helping himself to another marshmallow. 'Everything's better on the beach!'

Mandy could only agree with Josh. They were having a great time. If it hadn't been for the porpoise's uncertain future, Mandy would be perfectly happy. *Morveren* will *survive and join her family again*, Mandy told herself firmly. But the more she tried to convince herself of this, the less certain she felt. What if Morveren's injuries didn't heal? What if she became more stressed over the next two days? Mandy shivered. She didn't want to think like this but she knew she had to be realistic.

Joshua yawned loudly and Mandy realised that she was also feeling rather tired. It had been a very long and exhausting day. 'Let's draw straws to see who's doing first, second and third watch,' she suggested. She picked up a thin stick and broke it into three different-sized lengths. 'The smallest is for first watch,' she said, holding the pieces in her hand so that only the tops showed.

Josh drew the straw for first watch, Mandy for second and James for third.

'That means I'll have the pleasure of waking you up in the middle of the night, James.' Mandy chuckled.

James wasn't always at his best when he had to wake up very early in the morning!

'Why am I always the one who has to be woken up?' he sighed.

'Let's see,' said Josh, looking at his watch to calculate how long each shift should be. 'It's half past ten now. Let's say we each do two and a half hours. That will take us through to six tomorrow morning when the sun will already be up. Is that OK?'

'Fine by me,' said Mandy.

'So I'll be awake from half past three!' groaned James. He took off his glasses and rubbed his eyes. 'I'll be half dead by tomorrow night!'

Mandy felt as if she'd only just gone to sleep

when she heard Josh whispering to her to wake up. 'Is it one o'clock already?' she asked, sitting up in her sleeping bag. She could just make out the form of Josh, crouching in the entrance to the tent.

She wriggled out of the sleeping bag and, dragging it behind her, crawled outside. 'Is Morveren all right?' she whispered to Josh.

'I think so,' he replied. 'She's been very quiet the whole time.'

'Has she eaten again?' asked Mandy, slipping on her trainers.

Josh shook his head. 'Not that I noticed,' he answered. 'But I did doze off once or twice. I couldn't help it – I was so sleepy. So, maybe she ate when I wasn't looking.' He took off his shoes. 'See you in the morning,' he said and disappeared inside the tent.

Mandy shivered. It had been cosy inside the tent but out in the open the air was damp and cool. She wrapped her sleeping bag round her and went across to the rock pool. The silence on the beach was so acute that Mandy could hear the sand crunching loudly beneath her feet.

A sudden sharp blow from Morveren heartened

Mandy. At least the porpoise still seemed to be breathing robustly!

I'll sit up on top of the rock and watch her from there, decided Mandy. Not making a sound, she climbed stealthily up the cold granite mass. She kept low to prevent Morveren spotting her and crawled on to the top, then lay flat and gazed down at the porpoise.

Like a dark shadow, the broad shape of Morveren hovered in the still water. Next to her, a bright silver orb drifted and wobbled on the surface of the pool. It was the reflection of the full moon. *It seems more than just a reflection*, thought Mandy. *It's almost as if the moon is watching over Morveren too.*

Choo, came Morveren's blow again. The water began to ripple and Mandy saw that Morveren was stirring. Suddenly the porpoise swam forward. She reached the far end of the pool in a flash then flicked her smooth body round and streaked the ten metres to the other end. Then she started back again. Relentlessly, Morveren swam back and forth in the pool, churning up the water which slapped sharply against the sides as if to emphasise her desperation.

This is no good, thought Mandy anxiously. She'll exhaust herself and become even more stressed. I have to calm her down.

Quietly at first, Mandy started humming the tune of 'Over the Rainbow'. Right at that moment, she couldn't think of any other tune and it had worked once before to help Morveren relax. Now it would have to work again.

Gradually, Mandy hummed louder. *I wish I could think of another song – just for a change*, she thought.

The humming worked. Morveren slowed down. It was almost as if she was listening to the tune. She stopped swimming completely and lifted her head out of the water.

Mandy held her breath as the porpoise glanced from side to side. Then, to Mandy's delight, Morveren lunged for a piece of fish that was floating just in front of her. She swallowed the fish then grabbed another piece to one side of her.

Mandy's heart skipped a beat. Morveren was eating – and hungrily!

Mandy scanned the pool to see how much fish remained. She couldn't see any other pieces. *I'll fetch some more for her*, she decided. Shrugging off the sleeping bag, she slid silently down the rock and ran to the cool box.

The fish inside was still fresh and cold. Mandy dragged the box across the sand to the front of the rock pool. Leaning over the edge, she dropped a fish into the water.

Seconds passed, then Morveren suddenly swam across and swallowed the fish with one gulp before gliding back to the centre of the pool.

Shaking with excitement, Mandy put another fish into the pool. Again, Morveren streaked across and took the food.

Mandy was elated. *She's going to be all right*, she thought. She was even more delighted when she noticed that, instead of swimming away again, Morveren was hovering nearby. 'Do you want some more fish?' Mandy sang softly. Gently, she tossed another fish into the water.

Morveren caught it as it landed.

Much more of this and she'll be a performing porpoise! Mandy smiled to herself. She looked in the cool box. *Not a lot left*, she thought. *I'll leave the rest for later*.

Satisfied that Morveren wouldn't be hungry for a while, Mandy climbed back to the top of the rock. She slid inside the sleeping bag and settled down for the rest of her shift.

The time seemed to pass very quickly because, when she next looked at her watch, it was already nearly half past three.

Time to wake James, she said to herself. Reluctantly, she left Morveren and went over to the tent. She lifted the tent flap and stared inside. James and Joshua were sleeping soundly.

This isn't going to be easy, she thought, shaking James's leg gently.

James grumbled and turned over on to his side. For a moment Mandy considered leaving him to sleep and doing his shift for him. But then she realised that James would probably be very hurt if he missed out on looking after Morveren.

Mandy shook his leg again. 'James!' she whispered. 'Wake up. Morveren's waiting for you.'

'Huh?' grunted James.

'It's time for your watch,' Mandy said. 'Remember Morveren?'

'Morveren! Of course,' mumbled James, sitting up and reaching for his glasses which he'd put at the back of the tent.

'Are you *sure* it's already half past three?' he

whispered as he emerged, blinking, from the tent.

Mandy nodded. 'There's some orange juice if you need a drink,' she said.

James poured out a cup of juice for each of them and helped himself to a Cornish pasty that was left over from the picnic.

'You're not the only hungry one,' whispered Mandy mysteriously, as she watched James biting into the pasty.

'Sorry, Mandy,' apologised James. 'Did you want it?' He offered the pasty to Mandy.

'No,' she said with a grin. 'That's not what I meant. What I'm trying to tell you is that someone else has been having a midnight snack.'

James's eyes grew wide. 'You mean Morveren!' he exclaimed. 'Has she been eating?'

'Uh-huh. Like there's no tomorrow,' smiled Mandy.

James was on his feet in a flash. Suddenly he was wide awake! 'That's great news,' he said and ran over to the rock pool.

Mandy watched him climbing the big rock. The moon had set and for a moment James vanished as his shape merged with the darkness of the rock. Then he appeared again, on top of the rock, silhouetted against the sky.

Morveren's night-watchman, thought Mandy, as she saw James sit down and lean over to look at the porpoise below.

The raucous calling of seagulls woke Mandy next morning. She crawled out of the tent to find Joshua chasing the greedy birds away from the bucket of fish scraps.

'Just as well I woke up before they pinched it all,' he panted over his shoulder.

Mandy looked in the bucket. The gulls had eaten half of the fish.

'We'll need to find some more,' she said. 'Morveren started eating last night.'

Josh's face broke into a wide grin. 'Great!' he said. Then his face darkened. 'The trouble is we might not be able to find a lot more. Remember, we bought everything the village shop had.'

'Didn't Ed say he'd try to find some more scraps?' asked Mandy.

'That's what he *said*,' Josh muttered. 'But he doesn't always do what he says.'

Mandy hoped that this time Ed would stick to his word. 'Let's see if Morveren wants any more,' she suggested, picking up the bucket and heading for the rock pool.

James looked stiff and tired but he greeted Mandy and Josh cheerfully. He slid down the big rock and joined them at the front of the pool. 'She's been floating calmly – I mean logging – all night,' he reported.

'Hello, Morveren,' murmured Mandy.

The porpoise stirred.

'Hey! I think she knows your voice,' said James.

Mandy shrugged. 'Well, I did spend most of the night singing to her!' She handed the bucket to James. 'See if she'll have anything to eat.'

James dropped some scraps into the pool. For a minute, it looked as if Morveren wasn't interested as the fish drifted towards her. But all at once she seemed to make up her mind. She surged forward and swallowed the food eagerly.

'That's magic!' Joshua smiled. 'Just wait until Dad hears about this. He won't be so gloomy about her chances then.'

'Now all we need is a gigantic storm,' James said with a grin.

'And no more jetskis,' added Mandy.

'The best way to make sure of that is to start

the awareness campaign right now,' said Josh decisively. '*One* porpoise driven ashore is too many. We *have* to stop this from ever happening again!'

'So what are we waiting for? Let's get started!' Mandy declared. 'What are your plans?'

Josh stared out to sea for a moment. 'OK. Here's what we do,' he said. 'One of you stays here with Morveren and the other comes home with me to print out a leaflet about how jetskis and speedboats are a menace to the local wildlife. I've already made a start on it, we just have to run off some copies. We'll make photocopies of it at the village shop and give them to everyone we see.'

James elected to stay with Morveren. 'Mandy will know what to say in a leaflet,' he said.

Josh turned to Mandy. 'Then maybe you could have a look at what I've done already,' he said.

'Sure,' said Mandy. She took one more look at Morveren. 'See you later, little one,' she said then, grabbing her camera from the camp, she followed Josh towards the cliff path.

As they ran across Terry George's fields, Mandy remembered the heifer. *It's still early so I'll see to her on the way back,* she decided.

* * *

At the Gills' house they bumped into Janet Gill coming out of the front door.

'How is Morveren?' she asked, her blue eyes looking at them with concern.

'We think she's much better,' Josh told her. 'She's even taken some fish.'

'That's wonderful news,' said his mum. 'Let's hope she keeps it up.'

'She *has* to,' murmured Mandy.

Janet Gill smiled at her kindly. 'If positive thinking could rescue Morveren, thanks to you she'd have been out of that pool a long time ago!'

'It would be great if that was all it took,' said Mandy.

Mrs Gill turned to Josh. 'Have you come back for more supplies for your camp?'

'Not really,' said Josh. 'We're going to do a bit more work on that leaflet I started – the one to warn people to be aware of the porpoise nurseries.'

'We thought we should start the campaign before Morveren goes back to sea,' added Mandy.

'Well, I'm on my way to a council committee meeting right now,' said Janet Gill. 'If there's an opportunity, I'll raise the issue of the porpoises. Perhaps we could arrange for buoys to be placed at the edge of the cove where the nurseries are.'

'That would be a start,' said Josh hesitantly. 'But I don't know that buoys alone will make a difference – jetskiers and people in speedboats might just ignore them, unless we can make them feel bad about what they're doing.'

'Well, let's see if together we can make something happen,' said Janet Gill. She kissed Josh briefly on his cheek and hurried over to her car, pulling her curly dark hair into a ponytail as she went.

Mandy and Joshua went to the study and set to work. Mandy stared fiercely at the computer screen and thought hard.

'We must tell people that porpoises aren't the same as other marine mammals like dolphins, which enjoy bow-riding and playing in the wakes of boats,' she advised. Josh tapped rapidly on the keyboard, and sentences flashed up on the screen.

'And we must make sure we get across how dangerous jetskiing can be to marine wildlife if the riders don't take care,' she went on.

'Yes, that should be the most important

message,' Joshua agreed, nodding.

When they were satisfied with the wording, Joshua started to arrange the sentences in an eye-catching design.

'Have you got an image of a porpoise in any of the programmes on your computer?' asked Mandy. 'That would help attract people's attention.'

'I don't know,' said Josh. 'I'll have a look.'

'It's a pity your mum's gone out,' said Mandy. 'There's a picture of Morveren in my camera. She could have developed it for us and we could have used that for the leaflet.'

'You still *can* develop it,' said a voice behind them.

It was Ed. Mandy hadn't noticed him come into the study. 'I'll do it for you,' he offered. He leaned over Josh's shoulder. 'Strong words, those,' he said, reading the text on the screen.

'They have to be, to get through to people like you,' muttered Josh.

Mandy followed Ed to Janet Gill's tiny darkroom. As she watched Ed prepare the special chemicals and trays, Mandy wondered if the leaflet would influence him. *It has to*, Mandy told herself. *And we can probably judge from his reaction how other jetskiers will respond.* Like Josh, Mandy didn't think the marker buoys would make much of a difference on their own. The leaflet was probably their best chance of making jetskiers aware of the harm they were doing.

Ed slowly developed the enlarged photographs, sloshing the sheets of paper in liquid until a shadowy image appeared. Then, one by one, he held the prints up in the dim red light.

'This one's fantastic!' He laughed when he saw the shot of James with the sea swirling round him. 'I'll make a few copies so that we can all have one.' Ed continued to chuckle to himself as he sorted through the pictures. Then, suddenly, his laughter stopped and he became very quiet.

He was staring at one of the photographs. Puzzled, Mandy leaned over Ed's shoulder to see what had made him so serious. She gasped. 'That's amazing!' she breathed when she saw the picture.

It was the close-up shot of Morveren's gentle face. The picture said what all the words in the world could never express. Trapped and bruised in her rock pool, Morveren's heart was breaking.

'She looks so unhappy,' said Ed, and Mandy

noticed a catch in his voice.

She felt a surge of hope. If Ed was touched by the picture of Morveren, then surely others would be too?

Eight

'This will definitely have to go in the leaflet,' Mandy said, taking the damp photograph gingerly from Ed.

'Yes,' agreed Ed. 'That sad expression should melt a few hearts.'

'Let's hope people will take notice of what the leaflet says,' said Mandy, heading for the door of the darkroom. 'Otherwise more porpoises could end up on the beach.' She waited briefly, hoping for Ed to say he would keep away from the porpoise nurseries in Sennen Bay in future. But he said nothing as he set about clearing up the equipment. Disappointed, Mandy closed the door and went back to the study.

Josh was also very impressed with the photograph. 'It's exactly what we wanted people to see,' he said. 'Great work, Mandy!'

'It was just luck really,' smiled Mandy. 'Normally James takes much better photographs than I do.'

'Yes. Especially when you and I are almost being drowned by a big wave!' Josh grinned, referring to their drenching on the rock the day before. He placed the picture inside a scanner. 'I'll scan it on to the computer then transfer it to the leaflet.'

Within minutes the leaflet was printed out, with Morveren's beautiful face gazing out on the front page, and Mandy and Josh were on their way to the village shop to have it photocopied.

When the shop owner learned what the pamphlet was for, he offered to do the copies free of charge. His generosity encouraged Mandy and Josh enormously.

'Perhaps a lot of people will be that positive,' said Mandy, as they left the shop and began handing out the copies to passers-by.

Mandy studied the reactions of people when they received the leaflet. Some glanced through it quickly then put it in their bags or pockets to be read more closely, Mandy hoped, at a later stage.

A few took one look at it then tossed it into the nearest bin. Mandy was disappointed each time that happened. 'They're probably the ones who own jetskis or power boats,' she complained to Joshua. 'I feel like running after them and insisting that they read every word!'

However, there were many people who stopped and stared at the picture of Morveren then went on to read the text carefully, shaking their heads from time to time.

One elderly woman even turned back when she had gone some way down the street and called out to Mandy and Josh, 'Good for you! It's about time someone paid attention to our precious sea life. I'll tell all my friends to make their children and grandchildren aware of the problem.'

'Thank you,' Mandy called back. Then she turned to Josh and said, 'I'd forgotten about that.'

'About what?' asked Josh, handing one of the leaflets to a young boy skating past on a zippy aluminium scooter.

'That people would carry the message even

further by talking to others about it,' she said. 'Morveren's going to be famous!'

'Let's hope that's not until she's safely out to sea again,' said Josh. 'Even though we didn't say exactly *where* she is, people will probably start looking when they know she's somewhere nearby.'

'And it would take just one cliff walker or rock climber to discover her for the word to get out.' Mandy frowned. 'I hope the storm comes soon.' She looked up at the sky and then stared out to sea. It was a warm, cloudless day and there wasn't even a hint of a breeze. Could the weather forecast be wrong?

It's just the lull before the storm, she hoped, remembering how suddenly the first storm had come up. Nevertheless, she was anxious about Morveren. She hoped they'd soon finish handing out the leaflets so that they could get back to her. But they'd need to find some more fish first.

'Let's go down to the harbour now,' said Joshua, heading down a steep, narrow lane. 'We might find some jetskiers there.'

'I think we've found one already,' said Mandy. She had spotted Ed at the bottom of the lane. He

was coming towards them, carrying a big plastic bucket.

'I've managed to get some more fish scraps for Morveren,' he said, as they met halfway along the lane. 'I figured you'd be needing more by now.'

Before Mandy could thank him, Ed offered to take over handing out the leaflets. 'I'll help Josh so that you can go back to Morveren with the fish,' he said. 'Just as long as you can carry the bucket!' he added with a grin. 'There are quite a few kilos of fish in there.'

Mandy lifted the bucket. Ed was right. Morveren certainly wouldn't be going hungry today! 'I'll manage,' she said.

'I would have taken it down to the beach for you,' Ed went on, 'but I think it's important to get this leaflet out as soon as possible. And seeing as I know a lot of jetskiers, it makes more sense for me to give it to them.'

Mandy was astonished at Ed's co-operation. He had obviously been deeply shocked by the photograph. An idea suddenly came to her. Perhaps Ed should actually *see* Morveren. If the photograph had pricked his conscience, the sight of her in the flesh would be even more powerful.

'Why don't you spend the night with us at our beach camp?' she offered. 'Then you can meet Morveren.'

Ed looked pleased. 'I'd like that,' he said. He looked sideways at his brother. 'But I'm not sure Josh would want me there.'

'It's OK,' mumbled Josh. 'Seeing as you've done us a lot of favours, you can come down.' He explained which beach Morveren was on. 'But don't tell anyone else,' he warned his brother. 'We don't want the whole of Cornwall flocking there.'

On the way back to the secluded beach, Mandy stopped at Cliftop Farm to see how the heifer was doing. She met the farmer driving a tractor across a field.

'Jump up and I'll give you a lift to the barn,' he said. 'I've got something to show you.'

Mandy clambered up behind him. 'Thanks for the fantastic picnic yesterday,' she said as they bounced across the field to the farm buildings.

'Thank *you* for helping with the heifer,' said Mr George. 'She's much better now. In fact, I was able to let her back out with the rest of the herd this morning.'

'What about her calf?' asked Mandy, as they climbed down from the tractor and entered the barn.

'He's with the other calves. I'll feed him on formula milk in a bucket for a while,' answered Mr George. 'But talking of calves – what do you think of this?'

He pointed to a stall just ahead. Mandy peered over the half-door and saw a tiny, newborn calf resting in a heap of fresh straw. The proud mother stood alongside, dipping her head and licking her baby gently.

'It's gorgeous,' breathed Mandy. She never grew tired of seeing newborn animals – even though she must have seen hundreds before.

'Third one since yesterday,' said Terry George happily. 'And I think another two will be on their way soon.'

'There certainly are a lot of calves around at the moment,' grinned Mandy. 'Porpoise calves as well as bovine calves!'

'Porpoise calves!' exclaimed Mr George. 'What with all these calves appearing, I nearly forgot about Morveren. How is she today?'

'Much better,' said Mandy, as they left the barn. 'She even started to eat last night.'

'That's a good sign,' said Mr George. 'Let's hope she keeps it up.'

'Now we're just waiting for the storm so that, like your heifer, she can also join the rest of her – um – "herd", ' Mandy said, smiling.

Terry George took off his battered denim cap and ran his hands through his thinning hair. 'Better not get your hopes too high, though,' he said quietly. 'Porpoises are sensitive animals. You can never tell if they're going to give up or keep fighting.'

'Morveren's a fighter,' said Mandy firmly. 'And a survivor.'

'I hope you're right,' said Mr George, sounding unconvinced. 'Oh, by the way,' he went on, changing the subject, 'my wife picked up the picnic basket, it's refilled and waiting in the kitchen for you.'

Mandy left the farm feeling like a pack donkey. As she struggled down the cliff path with the bulky picnic basket and the heavy bucket of fish, a pair of seagulls circled her. Their beady black eyes were fixed on the fish in the bucket.

'No, you don't!' Mandy warned them loudly. 'This isn't for you. You're free to find your own food.'

James was glad to see Mandy – and the fresh picnic. 'You're just like those gulls, the way you're eyeing the food,' joked Mandy.

'Well, I *am* starving,' said James. 'I haven't had any breakfast, you know, and it must be nearly lunch-time already.'

'Let's feed Morveren first,' said Mandy. 'Then we'll eat.'

They carried the bucket over to the rock pool. As before, Morveren was floating silently just beneath the surface of the water.

'Has she been quiet all the time?' asked Mandy.

'Just about,' said James. 'She did swim back and forth a few times. I thought she was a bit anxious so I – er – sang a song to her again.' He blushed. 'I felt a bit of a fool singing all by myself on a deserted beach! Imagine if someone had sneaked up on me and heard me.'

'It's all in a good cause,' Mandy said, laughing. She dropped a piece of fish into the water. It floated into the centre of the pool then, as before,

Morveren grabbed it with one flick of her muscular body.

Mandy picked up a fish tail. She was about to toss it into the water when the porpoise shot across the pool and stopped just in front of Mandy. It was as if Morveren was waiting for the fish. Mandy felt a tingle of pleasure. Perhaps Morveren really *did* recognise her. Quickly she dropped the fish into the water. Without hesitating, the porpoise swallowed it in one gulp then swam off to the other side of the pool.

Mandy's face lit up. 'I wasn't expecting that,' she whispered to James. 'It's almost as if she came over to ask me for something to eat.'

'It was amazing!' said James, shaking his head in astonishment. He took another tail out of the bucket. 'Let's see if she'll do it again.'

He dangled the tail above the water but Morveren ignored both James and the food.

'Perhaps she's had enough,' Mandy said. 'Let's give her a break for a while.'

'Yes – and we can have *our* lunch,' James said with a grin.

'Not just yet,' Mandy said, turning to see Josh and Chris Gill walking across the beach towards them. 'We need to see what Chris has to say about Morveren first.'

Mandy and James waited anxiously as the two figures approached them. As Mr Gill reached the rock pool, he pulled himself on to the ledge and crouched down to watch Morveren. The porpoise floated motionlessly at the far end of the pool as if she didn't want to be seen.

Mandy bit her lip nervously as she waited for Chris Gill's expert opinion. The vet stared at the little creature for ages, then he stood up and slowly made his way round the pool towards Morveren. As he approached, the porpoise flicked her tail and swam away from the edge until she was just out of reach. Then she settled down again and appeared to be watching Chris Gill, who kneeled down and gazed at her too.

'It's like they're having a staring match,' James whispered to Mandy and Josh.

'If they are, Morveren will win,' said Josh. 'Dad's not all that patient!'

Eventually, Chris Gill straightened up and, with one last glance at Morveren, walked away from her along the rocks, then jumped down on to the sand next to Mandy. 'Well, as far as I can tell without physically examining her, the porpoise is looking quite healthy,' he said.

Mandy was overjoyed but she wanted to hear more. 'Does that mean she's definitely going to survive?' she asked.

Chris Gill folded his arms and shrugged. 'The fact that she's eating is a very good sign.'

There was a small ripple in the water as Morveren moved quietly back to the sheltered end of the pool.

Chris Gill went on. 'All we can do now is watch her and hope that, when the storm comes, she'll grab the chance to swim back to sea. I'll come back tomorrow to check on her again.'

When Chris Gill had left, Josh told Mandy and James he had some good news for them. 'Mum said that the local newspaper has promised to write a story about the campaign,' he said cheerfully as they sat eating the picnic lunch. 'And lots of people who read the leaflet seemed really concerned about the porpoises living in the cove.'

'So far, so good,' said Mandy. 'But I wonder what Ed's friends said when he gave them the leaflet.'

'We'll be able to find out soon,' said James, looking towards three tall figures on the cliff path.

Ed and two of his friends were making their way down to the beach. When they reached the camp, Ed glanced around quickly as if he was trying to see where Morveren was. Then he introduced his friends. 'This is Matt, and Dave,' he said. 'I hope you don't mind them coming too – especially as Matt is the only one with a tent.' He looked across at his own tent pitched on the beach.

'I suppose it's OK,' said Josh. 'Just as long as they're the only ones.'

Ed patted Josh playfully on his back. 'Come on, Josh. Lighten up,' he said. 'We're trying to help you. Look,' he went on, opening a large shopping bag, 'we've even brought down some food for a barbeque tonight.'

'That's nice of you,' said Josh with a trace of hostility in his voice.

Mandy understood Josh's hesitation. He needed more solid proof that Ed's apparent concern for Morveren was genuine.

Pherrh. A familiar, drawn-out puffing sound broke into the conversation.

'Was that Morveren?' asked Ed eagerly, looking in the direction the sound had come from.

'Yes,' Mandy said. 'Would you like to see her now?'

'You bet,' said Dave. 'I've never seen a porpoise close up.'

'That's because you . . .' began Josh, but Mandy quickly interrupted him. She didn't think more arguing would help matters.

'You'll have to be very quiet,' she warned. 'We don't want Morveren to be upset at all.'

As they peered over the edge of the rock pool, Ed and his friends were clearly overwhelmed by the sight of the isolated young porpoise.

'Dad said she had some skin wounds,' whispered Ed. 'Are they any better?'

'Nearly,' said Mandy. 'She's had a long-lasting antibiotic injection so she shouldn't get an infection.' She reached into the fish bucket, which she and James had left nearby. 'Keep back,' she told Ed and his friends. 'I'm going to feed Morveren but she might not take the fish if she spots unfamiliar people.'

They took a few steps backwards and Mandy dangled the fish above the water. Humming softly, she waited for Morveren to respond as she had done before.

For a while, the porpoise did nothing. Mandy wondered if she shouldn't just drop the fish and allow Morveren to find it later, when they had gone.

At that moment, the water round the little animal rippled slightly then, as quick as lightning, Morveren streaked across the pool. Mandy let go of the fish. At the same time, Morveren lifted her head and caught the food before it landed in the pool.

Josh's face broke into a huge grin. 'That's so cool,' he whispered. 'She'd never do that if she was still in shock.'

Mandy could almost see the load of worry lifting off his shoulders.

Ed and his friends looked at Mandy in awe. 'How did you get her to do that?' asked Matt.

Mandy shrugged her shoulders. 'By singing the same tune over and over again, I suppose,' she replied. Then she winked at Josh and whispered meaningfully, 'I haven't changed *my* tune, but I hope others have changed *theirs*!'

Josh laughed quietly, then, turning to Ed and

his friends, said, 'Luckily it looks like Morveren is going to survive after all and will be able to join her pod again.'

'Do we just pick her up and put her into the water when she's ready to go?' asked Dave.

'Definitely not!' said Josh, sounding alarmed. 'Don't forget, porpoises are very shy animals. If we pick her up, we could cause her more stress.'

James was dangling a piece of fish into the water but it seemed as if the porpoise had only bonded with Mandy. She steadfastly ignored James's offering.

'I guess Mandy has the better singing voice,' joked Ed when James finally gave up and let go of the fish.

'So how *will* she get back into the sea?' asked Matt. He seemed genuinely anxious to help Morveren return to the wild.

Mandy told them about the predicted storm. 'That's our best bet,' she explained. As everyone looked disbelievingly at the dead calm ocean, she added, 'If the tide doesn't swamp the rock pool again, then we'll have to go for plan B – the stretcher.'

Josh looked worried at the suggestion.

Mandy nodded at him in silent agreement. Although Chris Gill had said that a stretcher was an option, she didn't want to cause any more unnecessary stress to Morveren, especially when she seemed to be feeling better.

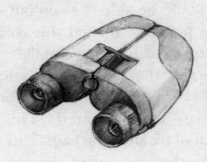

Nine

The storm! It's here! Mandy was woken by the loud whistling of the wind and the noisy flapping of the tent. She sat up in her sleeping bag and switched on the torch that Mrs George had put in the picnic basket. She looked at her watch. It was only two in the morning. They had decided not to watch Morveren all night, since she was so much calmer now.

A shiver of excitement ran through Mandy as she listened to the crashing of the surf on the beach. Here, at last, was Morveren's opportunity to return to her pod. Silently, Mandy prayed that

Morveren would be able to swim out of the rock pool. If the porpoise missed this chance, would she ever return safely to her family?

James stirred, then sat bolt upright, suddenly aware of what was going on outside the tent. 'The storm's here!' he exclaimed. 'This is it.' He wriggled out of his sleeping bag. 'This wind could probably rip the tent out of the sand,' he said. 'We'd better get out of here.'

'You mean we could be swept away?' gasped Mandy.

James' wriggling woke Josh, who immediately leaped into action. 'Let's see what's going on out there,' he said, scrambling into his waterproof jacket.

Mandy crawled out of the tent into pitch-black darkness. She could just make out the shadowy figures of James and Joshua, standing on the sand. Thick sea-spray swirled round them, clinging to their hair and clothes. There was no sign of the moon. The spray and low clouds had blocked it out. Once again, the weather had changed dramatically.

Mandy had a flashback to the previous night when, at exactly the same time, she had been sitting in bright moonlight on the big rock watching Morveren floating in the shimmering pool below. *I hope she's OK*, she thought, feeling a twinge of anxiety for the porpoise. *I'll go and check on her.*

'Ouch!' said James as tiny, stinging sand particles were blasted into their faces by a gust of wind.

Mandy turned her head away from the gale. 'We could do with Balaclavas and goggles,' she said, half closing her eyes to protect them from the sand and wind. She was about to set off for Morveren's pool when Joshua, who had ventured a little way towards the sea, shouted out from the murky gloom.

'Hey! The water's rising quickly,' he cried.

Mandy shone the torch towards him but even in the bright beam, he was only just visible in the sea spray.

'It'll swamp the tent soon,' Josh warned, reappearing out of the gloom. 'We'll have to move it to higher ground.'

'We'd better wake the others,' said Mandy, shining the torch at their tent. She'd have to see to Morveren later.

Josh ran over and opened the flap of the second tent. He called to Ed and his friends and warned them about the rising tide. In an instant, they were up and preparing to decamp.

It wasn't easy to dismantle the tents in the raging wind – and in the wavering light of a single torch.

'Hold tight,' shouted James, as a strong gust tugged at the canvas.

The tent billowed like the sail of a yacht at sea. Joshua wrestled it to the ground and sat on it while Mandy and James folded it up. They pushed it into its bag, then struggled up the beach, carrying all their belongings away from the thundering sea, which was quickly gaining on them.

Mandy flashed the torch up and down the cliffs. The beam picked out a broad ledge a short way up the cliff-face.

'That looks OK,' said Josh. 'Just as long as we can climb up there with all our stuff.'

Ed and his friends caught up with them and, one by one, they all hauled themselves up to the rocky ledge.

The wind drove into the face of the cliff,

sending tiny shards of shale spinning into the air.

'Bit of a wind trap, this ledge,' said Matt. 'It's worse than on the beach.'

'Yes, but count your lucky stars that at least the tide won't reach this far,' said Ed, spreading out his sleeping bag and getting into it. 'Mmm – not as soft as sleeping on the sand,' he muttered as he lay down and pulled the bag over his head, 'but I guess it's better to be dry than washed away!'

The others settled down for the rest of the night but Mandy knew she wouldn't be able to rest until she'd checked on Morveren. She scrambled back down the cliff on to the beach.

'Where are you going?' called James.

'To make sure Morveren's all right,' Mandy answered.

'Wait. I'm coming with you,' shouted James.

'And me,' Josh added.

Battling against the wind, they felt their way along the beach to the rock pool. Already the sea was lapping at the foot of the pool. Mandy hoped that the sound of the waves crashing so close would be a welcome sign to the porpoise.

Leading the way, Mandy climbed up the big

rock that overlooked the pool. She peered over the edge into the black water below. As her eyes became accustomed to the darkness, Mandy saw that the water was swirling around. It was like looking at a whirlpool!

At first Mandy thought it was the wind disturbing the water but, when she peered closer, she realised that Morveren was causing the turbulence.

'She's frightened!' Mandy cried, watching the porpoise swimming agitatedly round the perimeter of the pool.

'How do you know?' asked James, squinting at Morveren through his fogged-up glasses. 'Maybe she's excited because she knows this is her chance to go back to the ocean,' he said. 'What do you think, Josh?'

'I don't know what Morveren's thinking,' Josh replied. 'But I hope she isn't getting stressed again. Someone will have to fetch my dad as soon as it's light enough.'

'Well, let's see what we can do in the meantime,' Mandy said. 'Let's sing to her.'

'What?' James frowned. 'In this wind! She'll never hear us.'

'She will if we sing loudly enough,' Mandy insisted. 'Don't forget, marine mammals have very sensitive hearing.'

'I don't know if you can call it that,' said Josh hesitantly. 'They *do* use sound to work out their surroundings in the sea. It's called echo location. But I don't know if their hearing is as good out of the ocean.'

'Well, we'll just have to find out,' said Mandy firmly. After all, it would do no harm to sing to Morveren – even if she could hardly hear them above the noise of the storm.

At the tops of their voices, they began to sing their usual song.

'I'll be only too glad if I never hear "Somewhere over the rainbow", sorry, "seashore", again,' groaned James, rolling his eyes.

'I bet Morveren is thinking the same thing – if she can hear us,' Josh joked.

Gradually, Morveren seemed to relax. Her frantic laps of the pool slowed down and she began to drift more carefully from one end to the other.

'It worked!' Mandy said. 'She *must* have heard us. What else could have calmed her down?'

The storm had intensified in the short time they had been singing to Morveren. Mandy realised how dangerous it was for them to be out in the open while it was still so dark. Being a creature of the sea, Morveren was much safer from the heavy tide than they were. Now that Mandy knew Morveren was calmer, she felt she could leave her for the rest of the night.

As they turned to go, Mandy paused and gave the little porpoise one more look.

'Come on, Mandy,' called Josh. 'The water's rising really fast.'

'I know,' Mandy said. 'But I just have to say goodbye, in case I never see her again.'

'You'll see her again,' said Josh with certainty. 'She won't get out of there that easily – even if the sea does reach the pool. Remember, she only got in by accident.'

Josh's prediction was a big blow to Mandy. She had been so sure Morveren's ordeal was nearly over.

By daybreak, Mandy hadn't slept a wink. Anxious thoughts of Morveren, along with the roaring wind, had kept her awake all night. Mandy sat with her legs dangling over the ledge and looked towards the rock pool. The big granite rock hid the pool – and Morveren – from her view.

Pale daylight spread across the cove and revealed the full extent of the storm's rage.

'The sea's *huge!*' exclaimed James, sitting down next to Mandy.

Even though the wind had dropped considerably, the mighty Atlantic Ocean still surged and boiled in front of them. Gigantic waves crashed on the shore, sweeping foaming water all the way up the beach to the bottom of the cliffs. The spot where the tents had been pitched only a few hours before was completely swamped.

Josh crawled out of his sleeping bag and joined them. 'Just as well we broke camp in the middle of the night,' he said.

Mandy murmured in agreement. But her attention was on Morveren's pool. Had the sea risen to the level of the rock pool? And if it had, was Morveren still there? 'We have to see how Morveren is,' she said.

'And we need to send for Dad. I'll ask Ed to go,' said Josh. He looked down at the flooded beach. 'The trouble is, I don't think we'll be able to reach the pool,' he said with dismay.

James cupped his chin in his hand and surveyed the scene before them. 'I think I've figured out a way,' he said, after a while. He pointed down to the beach. 'Look over there. When the water washes back, you'll see a set of rocks leading to the big one next to Morveren's pool,' he explained. 'If we time it carefully, we should be able to get across them.'

'Like stepping-stones,' Josh agreed.

Mandy saw the black peaks jutting out of the swirling water as it rushed back to join the deep ocean. It was worth a try. If they were very careful, they wouldn't even get wet.

Murmuring behind them told them that Ed and his friends had woken up. And when Josh asked him and his friends to go home and call their dad, Ed readily agreed. 'We have to go back anyway,' he said. 'We've got some things to do in the village.'

'Yeah! For another trip on those blasted jetskis,' grumbled Josh under his breath as he, Mandy and James readied themselves to climb down the cliff. Then, more loudly, he said, 'Tell Dad to hurry. Morveren could be in danger again.'

'We'll phone him from Terry George's farm,' said Ed. 'That will speed things up.' He gave the three friends a concerned look. 'Be careful you don't put yourselves at risk too and end up falling into the water,' he warned them. 'It's pretty dangerous down there.'

'How can he warn us about dangerous water when he goes jetskiing in waves just like this?' muttered Joshua indignantly, clambering off the ledge to join Mandy and James on the narrow strip of sand.

Ed, Matt and Dave skilfully hoisted themselves up the rocky cliff-face. Within minutes they had reached the top and disappeared. Josh watched the waves closely. Timing it perfectly, as water flooded the beach then began to wash back again, he dashed across the rocks that James had seen jutting out of the water. Mandy and James followed him. Just as they clambered up on to the big granite mound at the poolside, another enormous wash of water swooshed up on to the shore, covering the stepping-stones completely.

'Phew!' said James, pushing his fringe off his forehead. 'That was close!'

Mandy held her breath as she reached the top

of the rock. The sea was almost level with the rock pool. Would Morveren still be there? Or had she managed to swim over the edge? Mandy looked down into the pool. 'She *is* there!' she said with mixed feelings. It was disappointing to see that Morveren was still trapped but, at the same time, Mandy was glad to see her again.

Morveren was swimming back and forth in the turbulent water. Huge waves crashed into the pool, forcing her against the rocks.

'She could hurt herself again!' Mandy cried in dismay. 'She *must* get out of there!'

But Morveren seemed to be making no attempt to leave.

'She's probably confused,' suggested Joshua. 'All we can do is sing to her again.'

While they sang to calm the worried porpoise, Mandy mentally willed Morveren to leave whenever a big wave washed over the edge of the pool. But every time the porpoise swam up to the rocks, she pulled back at the last minute, as if she was just too frightened to take the plunge.

Mandy could hardly bear to watch. And then, with a sinking heart, she saw that the tide had turned. The water was no longer washing over the stepping-stones that led to the big rock. Soon, the level outside the pool would be dropping too. 'It's too late!' she cried in despair. 'The tide's going out!'

They looked at the beach and were appalled to see that there was already a wide stretch below the cliffs where the water no longer reached.

'Here comes Dad,' said Josh with relief, pointing to the cliff path. 'He'll know what to do.'

Three figures were hurrying down the path to the beach. Mandy recognized Josh's parents and Terry George. As she watched them picking their way across the dry parts of the beach, Mandy couldn't help feeling that even Chris Gill wouldn't be able to persuade Morveren to leave the rock pool.

'She's looking pretty good,' said Mr Gill, when he had climbed to the top of the rock and seen Morveren swimming back and forth in the pool. 'Strong swimming motion. All she needs now is a bit of willpower to get herself out of there.' He looked at the rapidly receding water and frowned. 'But there's not much time.'

'Yes, it's now or never,' agreed Janet Gill quietly.

Morveren made a dash for the edge again as a

large wave crashed into the pool.

'Go, Morveren, go!' Mandy urged.

As before, the porpoise stopped just short of the edge. Briefly, she lifted her head and looked out to sea before swimming to the far end of the pool.

'It's as if she's afraid to make the leap to freedom,' said Janet Gill, shaking her head in disbelief.

Another enormous wave was rolling towards the rock pool.

'Look, Morveren!' cried Mandy. 'This one will help to lift you out. You *must* go now!' Her voice rang out above the thundering water. The little porpoise lifted her head and looked up at the rock where everyone stood. With an intense stare, she looked straight into Mandy's eyes.

Mandy's heart skipped a beat. 'Go, Morveren!' she cried again. 'GO!'

The mighty wave sent tons of water crashing into the pool. It washed over Morveren. Mandy bit her lip nervously. What if the wave drove the porpoise on to the jagged rocks?

And then, as the water begin to surge back out of the pool, Mandy saw that Morveren was swimming with the strong backwash towards the edge.

Mandy held her breath. She concentrated all her thoughts on the porpoise. *Don't stop this time*, she silently willed her. But at the back of her mind she expected Morveren to pull herself up again at the last second.

At the edge of the pool where the sea washed over, Morveren glanced back at her guardians.

Mandy thought she was about to turn round. But then, without hesitating, the porpoise wriggled over the rocky ledge and, with a strong flick of her notched tail, plunged into the water as it rushed back into the deep ocean. In an instant she had vanished.

It was all over. Morveren's ordeal had ended.

'She's out!' Mandy cried triumphantly, raising her hands in the air in delight. 'Morveren's going home!'

Ten

Everyone cheered and hugged each other on top of the big rock which for two days had acted like a watchtower for Morveren.

'It's almost as if she was waiting for us all to be here before she left,' Mandy said. 'I mean, she had lots of other chances to swim out.'

'Maybe she wanted her vet's permission first,' said Mrs Gill, laughing. 'After all, Chris did pronounce her to be looking fit and strong!'

'And I think she even said goodbye,' said Josh. 'That's why she stopped to look back at us.'

'Who can tell what was going through her

mind?' said Chris Gill. 'But one thing *is* certain,' he added, looking solemnly at Mandy, James and Josh. 'The antibiotics and ointment helped to keep her in good shape but without you three watching over her and keeping her calm, she may not have survived the shock.'

Janet Gill put an arm round Josh's shoulder. 'You three have done a wonderful job,' she said. 'Everything has turned out really well after all. I'm sure your day's been made, Josh.'

'You can say that again,' beamed Josh happily.

But, despite the joy of knowing that Morveren was, at that very moment, swimming out to sea, Mandy couldn't help wondering if everything would turn out so well in the long term. 'Will she be able to find her own family again?' she asked Chris Gill. She couldn't shut troubled thoughts of Morveren, hunting in vain through the turbulent sea, out of her mind.

'I'm sure she will,' said Chris Gill kindly, as he began to climb back down the rock. 'In fact, I should have told you that Terry spotted a small pod of porpoises swimming in this part of the bay yesterday.'

The farmer nodded in agreement.

'Does that mean they could be Morveren's pod?' asked Josh, his eyes lighting up.

'It's quite possible,' replied his father. 'They may have been looking for her. And who knows, they could even be communicating with one another at this very moment.'

Mandy felt a wave of happiness as she imagined the porpoises calling out to each other through the ocean depths. She was in awe of the way marine animals could pick up sounds under the water. As she pictured Morveren, listening for her mother's call, Mandy thought she, too, could hear a familiar noise.

She turned her head towards the noise and listened carefully. Even above the howling of the wind, she could hear it. A harsh, high-pitched drone. 'Oh no!' she cried out suddenly as she identified the sound. 'Jetskis! And they're coming this way.'

Josh froze as he listened for the noise. His eyes flashed with anger. '*That's* why Ed was so quick to leave this morning,' he said, punching a fist into the palm of his other hand. 'He and his mates wanted to ride the rough seas again.' He turned to his dad, who was climbing back up the rock to see what was happening. 'They're going to ruin everything,' Josh said. 'It's Ed and his friends – just when Morveren is on her way out to sea. He *knew* we were hoping she'd get out of the pool this morning. How could he *do* this?'

Chris Gill shook his head. 'I don't think we should jump to conclusions and assume it's definitely Ed. After all, he's not the only jetskier in the area.'

Appalled, Mandy watched as a group of about five jetskis came into view round the headland. They skimmed across the rough sea, heading straight for where Morveren could be swimming at that very moment.

Tears pricked Mandy's eyes as she thought about Morveren. What if she panicked again? *Just when she thought she was safe too*, Mandy said sadly to herself.

As the jetskis roared through the choppy water, Mandy suddenly realised that they were all the same colour – purple and white. 'That's definitely not Ed and his friends,' she said slowly, remembering that Ed's jetski was red.

'Mandy's right,' said Terry George, looking hard at the jetskis through the binoculars he had brought with him. 'Those look like the ones they rent out from the harbour.'

'Oh, no,' groaned Josh. 'Ed would have been bad enough but this just shows that our leaflet campaign hasn't worked. Even though we've told people about the wildlife in the cove, they still don't care about disturbing it.'

'I suppose that means the buoys I've been trying to arrange will also have little effect,' sighed Janet Gill, running a hand through her long, curly brown hair. 'There are always going to be people who ignore warning signs.'

'We'll have to warn them ourselves – now!' Josh blurted out, hotly. 'Morveren *has* to have a chance to find her family.' He started to jump about on top of the rock, waving his arms in the air. 'Hey!' he screamed at the top of his voice. 'Turn back, you're scaring the porpoises!'

James and Mandy joined in. They yelled as loudly as they could, trying to attract the jetskiers' attention. But it was to no avail. The riders couldn't hear them above the whine of the engines and the roar of the sea.

The riders were now performing stunts as they raced across the bay. Some of them rode ahead of big waves, just avoiding the foaming water when the waves broke.

'I wish they'd get dumped in the waves and damage their stupid jetskis,' muttered Josh crossly.

One of the riders turned into a large swell and zoomed up the face of it. At the top, the jetski took off into the air and was suspended there for a moment before it came crashing back to the surface of the water. The rider revved the engine and made the machine spin round in tight circles. Mandy winced. The deafening whine and the whirlpool action that was created were enough to frighten anyone – let alone a small, defenceless harbour porpoise looking for her family pod.

From the top of the rock, they all watched the scene in horror. There was nothing they could do to stop it. Mandy almost wished Morveren hadn't left the pool after all. *She was safe here at least*, she told herself.

'Hey! Stop that!' yelled Josh again, his voice now hoarse from shouting. Enraged, he began to shout at the jetskiers more loudly. But his protest was lost in the wind and the waves.

Mandy put her hand on his arm in sympathy. 'It's not going to help,' she said quietly. 'And even if they could hear us, I don't think they'd really care.'

'No,' agreed James, standing with his hands on his hips. 'They're having too much fun to think about animals.'

Josh hung his head and Mandy could see tears of frustration glistening in his eyes. She understood. She had also been in situations involving animals where she had felt absolutely powerless to do anything.

She sat down on the rock and hugged her knees against her. Who would have thought that, after surviving her imprisonment in the rock pool, Morveren would now have to deal with all this? It wasn't fair!

'Now what?' said Chris Gill suddenly.

Mandy stood up and looked towards the headland where Mr Gill was pointing.

'What's he doing?' pondered Josh's dad out loud.

A small boat had come into the bay. Its white wheelhouse and bright red hull stood out above the grey-green ocean. It was one of the local fishing trawlers, and it seemed to be going at full speed.

'I'm sure that's John MacDonald's boat,' said Chris Gill.

Mr MacDonald who Ed works for on Saturdays, Mandy thought.

Terry George peered at it through his binoculars. 'Yep! That's John's boat all right,' he said. 'I don't know any other that's called *The Puffing Pig*!'

'*The Puffing Pig*?' said James. 'That's an odd name for a boat.'

'Actually, "puffing pig" is the common name for harbour porpoises,' said Janet Gill. 'People think their blow sounds a bit like a puffing pig.'

'I suppose it does in a way,' said Mandy, hearing again in her mind the drawn-out puff of Morveren's blow.

Mr George was keeping a close watch on the boat through his binoculars. 'Surely John's not going to drop his nets in the bay?' he said, sounding puzzled.

'He'd better not!' said Josh angrily. 'Can you believe that a boat named after porpoises might now be making things worse for them?'

'We don't know that it is,' said Janet Gill, trying to soothe Josh.

Mandy looked at Josh and shook her head in sympathy. Sometimes people did do unbelievably thoughtless things when animals were around.

The trawler steered its way through the heavy swells with ease. It seemed to be heading for the jetskis and was gaining on them fast.

'It almost looks as if they're having a race,' said James.

Janet Gill shook her head. 'I can't imagine John MacDonald would be bothered with a bunch of jetskiers.'

'Hold on a minute,' said Terry George, his binoculars still trained on the boat. 'I can see a crowd of folk on the deck. They've got a loudhailer. One of them is holding it up to his mouth.'

'Let me see,' said Josh.

Mr George handed him the binoculars. Everyone stood in silence, anxiously waiting to learn what was going on.

'It's Ed!' announced Josh in surprise. 'And Matt and Dave. It looks like they're calling out to the jetskiers.' He handed the binoculars to Mandy.

She scanned the trawler until some people came into view. Josh was right. One of them was

Ed and he was definitely speaking into the megaphone. She lowered the binoculars and gave them to James. Then, as she watched, Mandy saw the jetskiers turn round and ride towards *The Puffing Pig*.

'It's all very mysterious,' said Janet Gill, as the jetskis pulled up alongside the fishing vessel and came to a stop, bobbing on the waves.

'Ed's leaning down and speaking to them,' said James. He gave the binoculars back to Josh.

Suddenly, to Mandy's amazement, the jetskiers began to move off. But instead of continuing on their destructive route across the bay, they headed back the way they had come – and this time they rode slowly and quietly, as if they were taking care not to disturb the unseen wildlife in the sea.

'They're leaving!' she cried ecstatically. 'Ed must have warned them about the porpoises.'

Joshua's face broke into a wide grin. His blue eyes sparkled with happiness. 'I think he's finally realised what it's like for the porpoises,' he breathed.

'That means the campaign wasn't a failure after all,' beamed James.

'No,' agreed Josh. 'It's worked better than I could have hoped. And Ed even used a "puffing pig" to come to the rescue of the real puffing pigs!'

Mandy took the binoculars from Joshua and trained them on the boat. Ed and the others were waving to them from the deck. She waved back, trying to signal how delighted she was.

'I can't wait to speak to Ed,' said Josh. 'To thank him for looking after Morveren like that.'

Chris and Janet Gill exchanged glances. 'At last, our sons agree about something,' Janet Gill said with a smile.

The Puffing Pig turned in a wide arc, then followed in the wake of the jetskis. Mandy watched it disappear round the headland. She breathed a sigh of relief. James and Josh were right. Their leaflet campaign *had* worked after all. From now on, the porpoises would be much safer. And what's more, thanks to Ed and his friends, Sennen Bay now had its own 'porpoise police force'!

Mandy focused the binoculars back on the bay and tried to imagine the reunion between Morveren and her family group. As she stared at the heaving ocean, she thought she caught a glimpse of something small and black, just beyond where the jetskis had been. She watched intently. The black dot was moving away from the shore. Mandy's heart leaped. Not far ahead of the black dot, she could make out several more dark shapes. *Dorsal fins*, thought Mandy. *They have to be.*

The tiny black shapes came together, then suddenly vanished. But Mandy had seen enough. She knew beyond a shadow of doubt that Morveren had found her family.

DOG IN THE DUNGEON
Animal Ark Hauntings 1

Lucy Daniels

Mandy and James will do anything to help an animal in distress. And sometimes even ghostly animals appear to need their help . . .

Skelton Castle has always had a faithful deerhound to protect its family and grounds. But Aminta, the last of the line, died a short while ago. So when Mandy and James explore the creepy castle the last thing they expect to see is a deerhound – especially one which looks uncannily like Aminta . . . Could it possibly be her? And what does she want with Mandy and James?